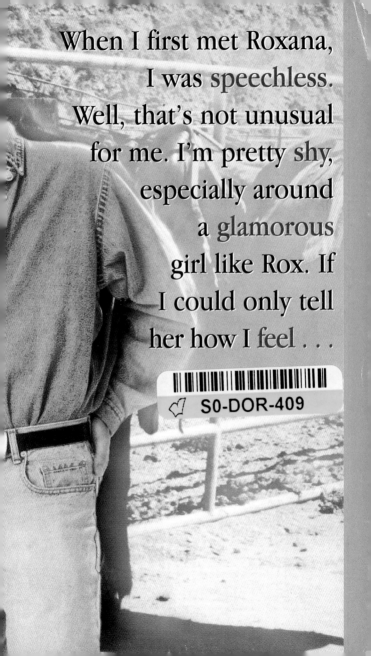

When I first met Roxana,
I was speechless.
Well, that's not unusual
for me. I'm pretty shy,
especially around
a glamorous
girl like Rox. If
I could only tell
her how I feel . . .

S0-DOR-409

How can I find the words . . .

Roxanna had touched him. With her own, actual finger. Without meaning to, Christopher raised his hand off the steering wheel and touched the place that she had touched. He left his hand there for a while, quite a while. And when he returned to the normal universe, he noticed she was looking at him, staring, really, and smiling in a new way that was happy but also mysterious and smugly pleased.

Her voice, when she spoke, was lower, quieter than before. "You seem to have gone away there for a few minutes . . . after I touched you," Roxanna said. "I hate to think what would happen if I ever kissed you, Christopher. You might just die of embarrassment."

"I reckon I might die, at that," he said. "But I'd die happy."

There. He had done it. He'd said it.

But it was too bad that Rox hadn't heard it. She'd already jumped out of the truck and was now nearly inside the school, having given up waiting for his response.

Don't miss any of the books in *Love Stories*
—a romantic new series from Bantam Books!

Love Stories

Listen to My Heart

KATHERINE APPLEGATE

BANTAM BOOKS
NEW YORK · TORONTO · LONDON · SYDNEY · AUCKLAND

RL 6, age 12 and up

LISTEN TO MY HEART
A Bantam Book / February 1996

Produced by Daniel Weiss Associates, Inc.
33 West 17th Street
New York, NY 10011

ISBN: 0-553-57013-7

Published simultaneously in the United States and Canada

Bantam Books are published by Bantam Books, a division of Bantam
Doubleday Dell Publishing Group, Inc. Its trademark, consisting of the
words "Bantam Books" and the portrayal of a rooster, is Registered in
U.S. Patent and Trademark Office and in other countries. Marca
Registrada. Bantam Books, 1540 Broadway, New York, New York 10036.

PRINTED IN THE UNITED STATES OF AMERICA

OPM   0 9 8 7 6 5 4 3 2 1

The author wishes to thank Edmond Rostand
and William Shakespeare, without whose
generous assistance I would have
had to invent my own plot.

Dedicated to Michael, who was only partly
the inspiration for Michael Serrano.

Chapter One

CHRISTOPHER MACAVOY UNBUTTONED his shirt, shrugged it off his broad shoulders and pulled the rolled-up sleeves down over his aching biceps. He hung the shirt neatly from the fence post he had just put up. He removed his worn straw cowboy hat and fanned his face. It was hot. Hot like it seldom got in western Montana, even now at the very tail end of August. His unruly blond hair was matted against the back of his neck. Sweat beaded on his forehead and ran down his neck to his chest, making the taut, tan skin shine in the blazing sun.

One more hole to dig, one more fence post to put in, and he would be done. He got a firm two-handed grip on the posthole digger and slammed it down into the hard, grass-bound soil. Twist left. Twist right. Squeeze and pull up. Repeat.

It was tiring work. Especially since he'd been at

it since dawn without a break, and it was now high noon. But he was the man of the Three Aces Ranch, and men worked.

The man, since his father had died two years earlier when Christopher was just fifteen. And even though his mother ran the business, and even though they had some hired help, Christopher had to set an example. He had to be the kind of rancher his father had been, a real rancher, not like these new folks who came out to Montana from Hollywood and Beverly Hills and bought ranches because they thought it sounded cool to talk about their "ranch" when they went on the David Letterman show.

Those people never had a callus on their hands. Christopher's hands were rough as sandpaper. Those people couldn't rope one of these fence posts, let alone a skittish calf from the back of a fast horse. Those people got their muscles from Soloflex machines and aerobics classes. The tight muscles in Christopher's chest and stomach and shoulders had been earned the hard way—from long hours of work.

He levered up the last fence post and dropped it into the hole with a satisfying "shoomp" sound. He shoved the fill dirt in around it and tamped it down with the heel of his boot.

Christopher looked down along the line of the wire fence that separated Three Aces property from the Pecos Pete Ranch.

"The Pecos Pete Ranch," Christopher muttered. Never mind the fact that the Pecos River was in Texas, not Montana. That didn't matter. The man who owned the PeePee, as it was derisively known by the local folks, was Craig Maslow, Hollywood director, producer, and megabillionaire, who had made some of his megabillions off a movie called *Pecos Pete.*

They raised llamas on the PeePee. Llamas. At least they had given up trying to raise ostriches, after several had frozen solid during the first winter. And now, rumor had it, Maslow was looking to run a small herd of zebras.

Which was one reason Christopher was mending this fence. No one wanted to find out what would happen when good Montana cattle and sheep came face-to-face with Hollywood llamas and zebras.

Still, I can't rightly blame them for wanting to come here, Christopher thought as he leaned on the posthole digger. He hadn't seen much of the world, except through TV and books, but he was confident that this must be one of the most beautiful places on earth.

He was standing in a vast expanse of gently rolling grassland, prime grazing land, nestled in a fortunate valley. It extended far to the northern and southern horizons. To the east, at the very limit of his sight, were mountains, gray and hazy in the far distance. But those were faraway, safe, benign mountains. Someone else's mountains.

His mountains were much closer. They rose in

3

the west, straight up like a wall built across the prairie. The lower slopes were covered by juniper, ponderosa, and lodgepole pine, broken up by high pastures that were bright with wildflowers in the spring. But the peaks of the mountains were bare as bone, jagged and sharp, like cruel teeth that seemed to be trying to rip a hole in the sky.

The last drops of the melting snow fed a stream that leapt and skidded down the mountain, cut a deep, narrow channel across the Maslow ranch, and broadened upon reaching the Three Aces. Just down the hill from where Christopher stood, the stream formed a little pond in a hollow of the land. A small stand of sandbar willows and birch trees bordered the pond, along with bunched serviceberry and chokecherry bushes.

It was very hot. Christopher realized that he was very sweaty. And, he knew, the water would be very cool. Very cool and wet and refreshing.

Christopher tossed the posthole digger in the back of his yellow Ford pickup truck and walked down to the water. He still had just the slightest limp in his walk, a stiffness in his left thigh where, a few weeks earlier, a bull had encouraged him to move a bit faster.

The shade of the trees and the sound of the water gurgling and chortling to itself brought a smile to his lips.

Christopher sat down on the grassy bank overlooking the pond. He pulled off his muddy boots, peeled off his socks, and stuck them inside. Then he stood up and stripped off his Wrangler jeans and his boxer shorts and sauntered to the water's edge. He'd been skinny-dipping in this pond since he was a little boy. In those days he'd had a rope hooked up to an overhanging branch so he could play Tarzan and swing far out over the water before plunging in.

Maybe he should rig up another rope one of these days.

The water was a delicious thing as it encased his hot, weary flesh. He groaned in pure pleasure and let himself submerge until the chill water closed over his head. Only then did he realize he was still wearing his hat. He looked up from below the surface and saw it floating there, an oval-shaped boat, sunlight gleaming through every gap in the straw weave.

His laughter exploded in bubbles and he surfaced, still laughing. He stuck the hat over his now-cooled face and lay back, floating on the surface, hovering between hot and cold, resting his sun-seared eyes beneath the relative darkness of his hat.

This might be his last dip in the pond for this year. Tomorrow was the first day of school, signaling the onset of autumn. Autumn came hard and fast in Montana and was soon displaced by winter.

First day of school. A chance to see all the friends he seldom saw during the summer, except in town at the feed store.

A chance to see *her*.

"Don't start thinking about her," he muttered. "Or you'll never get any work done."

But he did think of her. *Had* thought of her often over the last year. Tomorrow he would see her again. And this year it would all be different. This was his senior year. Time was running out.

He had two things to deal with right at the start of the year. The first school dance would be on Friday, and he was determined to ask her to go with him. The next weekend came the Longhorn Rodeo, the last of the season. And he was determined to make his first ever qualifying bull ride, having failed on his previous attempts.

It felt like a lot to handle. School, chores, a girl, and a bull. The first two were just hard work. He could handle hard work. The last two were terrifying. Although he did realize there was a certain irony in being as afraid of a hundred-and-ten-pound girl as he was of a fifteen-hundred-pound bull. Actually, *more* afraid. After all, the bull could only kill him.

Well, he told himself, best not to get to worrying. Worrying never got anything done, and he still had a lot of work to do.

He stuck down a leg and felt the bottom no more than a few feet beneath him. Mud squished between his toes. He stood, removed the hat from his face, stuck it on his head, and felt his heart come to a complete stop.

He was not alone. Someone was standing on the bank, looking at him.

A *female* someone.

A female someone he knew.

Her.

6

Christopher gulped. In a flash the hat went from his head to a lower location.

"I'm sorry, did I startle you?" asked Roxana Maslow. Everyone called her Rox. When they spoke to her, which Christopher never really had.

Christopher gulped again. He started to say something . . . or at least he started to think of something he *might* say if only his brain were connected to his mouth. Instead he just held on tight to his hat.

"I didn't realize anyone was down here," Rox said.

He nodded, confirming that he was, in fact, here.

"I wasn't spying or anything," she said, as if he had accused her.

He shook his head from side to side. No, he hadn't meant to accuse her of spying.

"I really didn't see anything," she said. "Much."

A small whimpering noise escaped from his throat, a combination of embarrassment and frustration. Frustration that he still could not think of a single word to say to Rox Maslow, even though most folks would think that this amounted to an introduction of sorts.

But he had never been able to say anything to Rox Maslow. The first time he had seen her was a year ago, when she'd arrived in Longhorn, Montana, and begun attending school. Christopher had never exactly been one of those charming, glib type of guys. Even with girls he'd known his whole life, his conversations seemed to consist almost entirely

7

of yes, no, uh-huh, and various grunts.

But with Rox, he had never even gotten that far.

People said he was a young man of few words. In Montana that was a major compliment, a sign of maturity. But Christopher knew better. He wasn't mature, he was terrified. Terrified of all females except his mother. And of all the females alive on planet Earth, it was Rox Maslow who terrified him most.

She was the most beautiful creature he had ever seen. It hurt him to look at her.

She was wearing a short, wispy calico dress that, with each breath of breeze, lifted and fretted and pressed against the contours of her body. Her legs were long, bare, perfect from the hem of her dress down to the tops of the cowboy boots she wore. She brushed the waves of her long, reddish-brown hair out of her eyes with a casual gesture and smiled.

"You know, we *are* neighbors," Rox said. "Although I guess this is your property, so maybe I shouldn't have come over without asking permission. I'm never sure what the rules are, even now."

And Christopher said, "Rox, you are welcome on the Three Aces anytime you'd care to grace us with your presence. I'd sooner object to a visit from an angel. You are as welcome here as sunlight, as a blue sky, as welcome as the air I breathe, because even though we've never spoken, I have loved you from afar. You fill my dreams, you . . ."

Or at least that's what he would have liked to say. What he actually said was, "Unh."

"You're saying I shouldn't be here?" Rox asked.

"No. Ma'am."

She smiled. She had a smile that made his knees quiver.

"Are you saying I shouldn't come here ever, or just when I might run into you skinny-dipping?"

Christopher swallowed hard again. "That last part."

Rox nodded. "Well, I apologize for intruding on your privacy. I'm still getting used to life here. I guess in California people are a little more . . ." She stopped herself, as if she thought she was running on too long. "I apologize," she said simply.

Christopher jerked his head in a way that was part acknowledgement, part forgiveness, part cool indifference, and ended up looking like a nervous twitch.

"Well, I guess I'll see you at school," she said. She turned and began to walk away. "Of course, I doubt I'll see quite this much of you."

Her sweet laughter hung in the air long after she was out of sight. And for several more minutes Christopher just stood there, still clutching his cowboy hat and wanting to drown himself. It wasn't so much the considerable embarrassment of being found naked (although that hadn't helped). It was more the realization that on his first real face-to-face interaction with Rox Maslow, he had sounded like a complete simpleton.

"Just kill yourself and get it over with, Christopher," he said miserably.

Only he couldn't really kill himself. Not with so much work to do.

9

"Okay, *that* didn't work," Rox muttered to herself as she passed through the broken segment of fence back onto her own family's land. "In fact, that was basically a disaster. Like I was supposed to know he'd be skinny-dipping?"

In her imagination the scene had happened very differently. In her imagination, Christopher had been resting beneath a tree, thinking, daydreaming . . . perhaps daydreaming about her. And when she had appeared, he had smiled and, in his shy, understated way, let her know how happy he was that she had made the first move to bring them together.

Then they had talked and talked and discovered that they had a lot in common, despite coming from two entirely different worlds. Maybe there had even been a little kiss, just a brief brushing of his lips over hers.

She savored that image for a moment.

Imagination was a wonderful thing. Too bad reality and imagination hadn't gotten together.

Rox shaded her eyes from the sun and looked around till she spotted him—Drifter, her horse. She gave a sharp whistle—she had recently mastered the art of whistling with two fingers stuck in her mouth—and Drifter cantered toward her. He was a smart horse, a quarter horse like the locals rode, a different breed from the pampered thoroughbreds her father insisted on raising.

"Hey, boy," she said, patting his broad brown neck. "Guess what? You know my brilliant plan? It didn't exactly work the way it was supposed to. Nope."

Rox swung up into the saddle, gasping at the heat of the sun-warmed leather on her bare thighs. "Ahyah! Oww. Whoa. Bad idea. Remind me, Drifter, next time you see me try to ride in a dress. Remind me it's a bad idea."

She turned Drifter toward home and set off at a comfortable walk. It was more than a mile to the house, but she was in no hurry. She wanted time to think. And for Rox, thinking usually meant talking.

"Thing is, Drifter, I don't know what it is, but I can't ever seem to just forget him. Do you know what I mean? Maybe not, since you're a gelding. Sorry to bring that up. I'm just saying, if he were just some guy, I'd shrug it off. I'd figure, okay, so he's not interested. No biggie."

Only Christopher wasn't just some guy, Rox knew. She had first seen him a year ago, at the start of their junior year, when she had just moved to Longhorn from L.A. She hadn't fallen in love with him at first sight. But even then he had caused a sensation like the minor earthquakes that were always rattling windows back in Los Angeles. And throughout the year her fascination with him had grown. As she had come to love Montana, he had come to be Montana for her. Or maybe it was the reverse. Either way it was more than just that. It was something deeper, something way, way deep down inside of her, like a voice that kept saying, "He's the one, he's the one," over and over.

Her best friend, Darby Todd, said it was because Christopher was unobtainable. Darby's theory was that Rox only wanted what she couldn't have, and she couldn't have Christopher because he was from a different world. They were practically a different species. For example, Darby pointed out that Christopher did *not* talk to his horse. In fact, there was some doubt that Christopher ever talked to anyone, whereas, according to Darby, Rox seldom shut up.

"Darby's full of it," Rox told Drifter. "She thinks everything is psychological. Besides, who says I can't get together with Christopher? It's going to happen. By the time of the first school dance. I just haven't figured out how."

Chapter Two

THE RADIO ALARM clock went off at 4:30 A.M. the next morning. Tanya Tucker, singing "We Don't Have to Do This."

"Yes, we do," Christopher grumbled. "We definitely do have to do this." He was now on his school year schedule, starting an hour earlier than usual.

He rolled out of bed, stood up, and with one eye still glued shut, searched in the dark for his jeans. He would shower later, after his morning chores and before school.

"Morning, Christopher," his mother said when he appeared in the kitchen. She had been up for half an hour already, and had coffee and juice on the table, bacon draining on paper towels, golden hash browns in a heap, and three eggs frying in a pan. CNN was on the little TV on the counter, with the

13

volume low. This early breakfast was just for him. Duke and Elmont, the ranch's two aging cowboys, would be by in another half hour to stoke up for the day's work ahead. Duke and Elmont were the full-time hands. Other younger hands came and went on a part-time basis.

Christopher gave his mother a quick peck on the cheek and sat down heavily at the table.

"First day of school today," his mother said as she slid the eggs onto his plate.

"Yes, ma'am," Christopher agreed. He gulped alternately at the coffee and the orange juice.

"Looking forward to it? Your senior year?"

Christopher thought for a moment. Was he looking forward to it? He didn't feel strongly one way or the other. So he said nothing.

His mother winked and gave him a smile. "I pity the poor woman you end up with someday," she said. "Just like your father—you spend words like they each cost five dollars."

Christopher laughed. It was a regular joke between him and his mother. But then, remembering the scene at the pond with Rox, he added, "I reckon Daddy always got around to saying the important things."

His mother met his eyes and then she looked away, at the little framed picture she kept above her sink—a man with a big, confident smile, his hat cocked at an angle. "Yes, I suppose he did at that," she said softly to the picture of Christopher's father.

"I'm thinking of signing on for the rodeo,"

Christopher said. "I have the fee all saved up."

"That's your decision to make," his mother said, carefully neutral.

"By the time he was my age, Daddy had two qualifying rides," Christopher said.

"And three broken ribs," his mother said.

Just the same, Christopher thought, it wasn't rodeo that had killed his father. It was a combine accident. He'd been cutting hay, not riding bulls. "I best get going," he said.

The Three Aces was only nineteen hundred acres, a little over a sixth as big as the Pecos Pete. But unlike the PeePee, the Three Aces was a working, functioning, barely profitable enterprise, with not quite four hundred head of Hereford-Angus cattle, a troublesome herd of Targhee sheep, enough hogs and chickens to supply the ranch's own needs, acres of hay and wheat, a small potato patch, and a half dozen good horses.

All the animals needed feeding, watering, cleaning, medicating, gelding, shearing, currying, moving, branding, rounding up, or some combination of those. All the crops needed planting, fertilizing, spraying, and harvesting. The tractor, the combine, and the trucks were all old and needed constant coddling. The barn and the house and the miles of fences all needed repairing. And Christopher was responsible for doing a good portion of this never-ending workload.

In fact, a good portion of it had to be done between 4:30 and 6:45, at which time he would shower, change clothes, grab a thermos of coffee and a huge roast beef sandwich for the trip, give a wave to Duke and Elmont, and make the hour-long drive to the town of Longhorn.

But when the weather was fine, as it was this morning, the drive was sheer pleasure. He drove into the rising sun, just a glow hiding behind the mountains and casting the sheer mountain face into shadow. He'd rolled down the windows in the truck, even though the air was chilly, and he drove fast along the single-lane dirt road, staying ahead of the dust cloud his tires kicked up, enjoying the smell of hay and earth, and the sound of the engine and the tires on gravel.

First day of school. Senior year. A lot to think about this year.

His mother wanted him to go to college. She said the modern rancher needed a good education. But Christopher wasn't so sure. It would cost money to attend college, and it would mean either a hundred-plus-mile commute to Bozeman or, more likely, moving there full-time. He could just about manage a hundred miles each way when the weather was like this, but it was seldom like this. And if he went to Bozeman, could his mother afford to keep the ranch going without him?

The dirt road joined the paved county road at the top of a gentle rise. There was traffic along the county road—as much as a vehicle every two minutes—about equally divided between cars, pickups, and farm machinery.

Christopher stopped to take a look back over his shoulder. It was the high point of the drive. He could see the house, the barn, the sheds—tiny, pristine buildings, like frail lifeboats riding on a sea of low, rolling hills. There was mist in all the low places, mist clinging to the lovely birch trees his great-grandfather had planted to shade the house. His great-grandfather had won the ranch in a card game. Won with three aces.

It was the same scene he had looked on many times, and yet it would never grow dull for him. Each day there were differences, as the wildflowers bloomed and faded, as the crops ripened and were harvested, as the valley went from green to gold to snow white.

Off to the north, up in Canada, winter was already waking up, preparing for the relentless march to the south. It made this green and fertile vision all the sweeter, knowing it would soon be gone.

In a few months the pond where Rox had spoken to him would be frozen, all but a channel through the middle where the current ran fast enough to keep from icing up.

That would have been better, Christopher thought. If she had come to him when the pond was frozen. He wouldn't have been so embarrassed then. That was why he'd acted such a fool—embarrassment. Well, who wouldn't be embarrassed? And it had cost him his one big chance to . . .

To what? he wondered. To win her over with his sparkling wit? Not hardly.

Someone said that Rox Maslow had gone out with a famous actor from a TV show at one time. At least that was the story. Anyway, one thing he could be sure of was that she was from a world where guys drove Porsches, not pickups. And where 4 A.M. was a late night, not an early morning.

Christopher pulled onto the county road and headed northwest toward the town of Longhorn, still thirty-five miles away. He'd been driving for just ten minutes when he saw a car pulled over onto the shoulder of the road. The hood was raised and someone was leaning back against the trunk.

From a distance Christopher recognized the car before he recognized her. There weren't a lot of red Mazda Miatas in the area.

He had to stop, he knew that. It would have been entirely unneighborly, not to mention ungentlemanly, to drive by and leave her standing out here, twenty miles from the nearest gas station or phone.

So he knew for sure that he had to stop. Only the thought of trying to speak to Rox Maslow, so soon after the debacle of the previous day, made his throat tighten up and his heart pound and his head buzz.

He pulled off onto the shoulder of the road and came to a stop just behind her. She was wearing a dress much like the one the day before, only now she had a baggy sweater over the top to ward off the early morning chill.

In the pearly, lavender light of morning she

looked beautiful and vulnerable and tough all at once. He would, at that moment, have given everything he owned to be able to think of one single intelligent thing to say to her.

He climbed out of the cab and reflexively touched the front of his hat out of respect for a lady.

"Morning," he said, forcing the word out through a dry mouth.

"Oh, good morning," she said. "There, um, is something wrong with my car."

He nodded. When he stepped closer, he could see that one of the tires was flat. No big problem. All he had to do was replace the flat tire with the spare. It wouldn't take five minutes. Surely he could manage not to make a tongue-tied fool of himself for five minutes.

"I'll be needing to get the spare out of the trunk," he said, jerking his head convulsively at the trunk.

"The spare?" she repeated. An awkward smile. "I don't think I have a spare tire. I took it out to make room in the trunk. It's kind of a small trunk. I like the car, but really, the trunk is kind of small."

Christopher was stunned. First, because it was hard to imagine anyone—even someone from Hollywood—not knowing that you'd need a good spare in the vast open distances of Montana. But worse by far was the realization that he didn't know what to say or do about the situation.

He said, "No spare?"

"I'm afraid not," she said. "Nope."

He tried to get his brain to think of what he could say next, but at that moment Rox happened to brush the hair out of her eyes, combing it back with her fingers. That simple event annihilated Christopher's train of thought and allowed only one idea to form: the idea that he wanted—wanted with a desperation and intensity that rocked him to the core—to touch her hair.

"So . . ." she said, waiting.

He snapped back to reality. He swallowed hard. "So, um, I guess you best ride in with me," he said, sounding like he was announcing the date of his own execution.

"That would be sweet, if you could give me a ride," she said. "I can call my house from school and my dad can send someone for the car. It shouldn't be any problem, and then someone can pick me up after school."

"My truck is . . ." He jerked a thumb back toward his truck, indicating its location. *Like she missed it,* he chided himself. *It's a great big old yellow pickup truck, Christopher. I think maybe she's noticed it standing there.*

"Let me just get my books," Rox said. She ran around the side of the little red car and leaned in through the open window. Her skirt rode perilously high and Christopher quickly turned away, feeling just a little disapproval that she would dress so provocatively. And yet not too much disapproval.

Seconds later they were on the road again, side by side, in a cabin that now seemed to be filled with nothing but Rox's bare legs and Rox's perfume and the easy sound of Rox's voice.

She was there, right beside him, *in* his actual truck. If only he'd known; he would have cleaned it up.

"I really appreciate this," Rox said.

"Yes, ma'am." He was clutching the wheel with both hands and scowling.

Rox laughed. "What's with the 'ma'am'? You don't call every girl ma'am, do you? I mean, how about Cassie and Julia and Kate and all those other girls at school? You don't call them ma'am."

"No, ma'am."

"Well then, why me? Call me Rox, or Roxana, if you absolutely have to. I prefer Rox. It sounds more . . . you know, more unique, more independent."

Had that been a question? He tried to analyze it. The sentence had contained several elements. At least one was a question.

"So," she said, "you didn't answer. Why call me ma'am? What am I, something special?"

Special? Only in the way that beauty, purity, grace, and perfection were special. Special only in the way that the most profound happiness, the greatest joy that could be experienced, the—

"So what I'm saying is, call me Rox, okay?" she said.

He ducked his head in a jerky little nod of agreement.

"Was that a yes?"

"Yes, ma'am. I mean . . . Rox."

21

"See? That wasn't so hard," she said. "You know, you don't have to be embarrassed over yesterday."

A wave of dread swept over him. Yesterday. He had managed, in the agony of the moment, to forget yesterday. Now she had said the word—*yesterday*. Which meant she was remembering it. Which meant that right now, at this very moment, she was thinking about him stammering and blushing and clutching his cowboy hat like it was the last life jacket on the Titanic.

"See, now you're blushing," Rox pointed out.

That was too much. Men did not blush. Especially cowboys. "No, ma'am. I mean . . . Rox."

She laughed gaily. "I'm not blind. I know a blush when I see one. It's going right up your neck."

And then, to illustrate her point, she ran her finger from his collar to his chin.

She had touched him. With her own, actual finger. Without meaning to, he raised his hand off the steering wheel and touched the place that she had touched. He left his hand there for a while, quite a while. And when he returned to the normal universe, he noticed she was looking at him, staring, really, and smiling in a new way that was happy but also mysterious and smugly pleased.

Her voice, when she spoke, was lower, quieter. "You seem to have gone away there for a few minutes, after I touched you," she said. "I hate to think what would happen if I ever kissed you, Christopher. You might just die of embarrassment."

They had reached the town and were threading their way through the cluster of cars arriving at the school, a mix of dusty pickup trucks, Jeeps, Broncos, and the sleek foreign cars of the California kids.

Christopher found a parking place and pulled into it. He turned off the key. He stared hard at the steering wheel, steeling himself to say the words that had leapt into his mind with the speed of crippled sloths, then made their way even more slowly down to his mouth.

"I reckon I might die, at that," he said. "But I'd die happy."

There. He had done it. He had said it.

It was only too bad that Rox had already jumped out of the truck and was now nearly inside the school, having given up waiting for a response.

Chapter Three

THE FIRST DAY of school, Rox thought glumly. She stopped just inside the big double doors and stared down the hallway. Gray lockers, dirty light blue cinder block walls, glaring unnatural florescent lights overhead. A smell that was composed of Lysol, chalk, mildewed books, cafeteria tamale pie, and unwashed gym uniforms. The sound of too many loud voices—shrieks of exaggerated delight and shouted hellos and laughter.

Someone had strung a banner across the intersection of the two hallways. It read Welcome Returning Students.

Welcome back to hell.

Okay, *not* hell, she corrected herself. Just high school. The difference being that she was pretty sure there were no pep rallies in hell.

The pleasant, almost tingling feeling that had

lingered from her ride with Christopher began to fade.

At least she was a senior now. That was good. That meant the end was in sight.

She was jostled by a pair of cheerleaders rushing down the crowded hallway.

"Hey," she protested.

One of the cheerleaders, a girl named Julia Ardmore, paused just long enough to give her a disdainful look, complete with curled lip and contemptuous snorting sound.

"Nice to see you again, too, Julia," Rox yelled after her.

The cheerleaders were a stronghold of the "locals," the *real* Montanans, as they saw themselves. The cheerleaders, the football and basketball teams, the 4-H, the After-School Bible Study Group, the various rodeo interest clubs, and, for some reason, the chess club. Each was an all-locals organization. No outsiders need apply.

The locals were easily spotted in the crowd—school football jerseys, bad haircuts, Caterpillar caps, Western shirts with pearl snaps, Wrangler jeans—everything inexpensive but clean and neatly ironed.

There were no clubs or organizations for the outsiders—the "Hollyweirdos," as the locals had dubbed them. But they could also be easily spotted in the milling crowd—professional haircuts, expensively downscale clothes with not a crease in sight, black-and-silver Raiders jerseys, Levi's and J. Crew jeans, expensive watches, multiple-pierced ears.

The outsiders were no more than 15 percent of the student body, just thirty or forty kids total, and most of them were not from Hollywood, or even California. Most were the kids of people who had come to Longhorn to provide services to the Hollywood people and the tourists who followed them. They were the kids of people who sold cappuccino and biscotti at the new coffee shops, duck pizza and truffle risotto at the trendy new restaurants, three-hundred-dollar shoes and five-hundred-dollar sweaters at the new clothing shops on Main Street. But all (even the ones who were just from Missoula) were identified with the new intruders. All were the enemy, as far as many of the locals were concerned.

Rox Maslow had tried not to be identified with the California clique. But her father represented the absolute epitome of the Hollyweirdo invasion. The fact that her father commuted back and forth to L.A. by private jet, traveled the area in a chauffeur-driven Land Rover, and refused to let deer hunters cross his land hadn't helped. The fact that her mother and father were divorced, and that her mother was an actress now remarried to another actor who had been married four previous times . . . that didn't help, either.

Rox had done what she could. She had kept quiet about being a vegetarian. Vegetarianism was not popular in this area of cattlemen. She had dressed simply and fairly inexpensively. She had opted for a relatively cheap car, instead of the BMW that some expected of her. She did not bring little bottles of Evian water to school with her, like some of the kids. She did not even mention that she had spent a big part of summer vacation with her mother on a movie set in Thailand. And she never, ever talked about her father or showed off by dropping the names of the celebrities who often visited the ranch.

She had even tried to enjoy Garth Brooks's music. She didn't enjoy it, but she had tried.

But every effort had ended up like her two attempts to get closer to Christopher—as pointless as trying to talk to one of the cows.

"Steers," she corrected herself sharply. "Steers, not cows."

"Noooo, these aren't steers. These are people. Of a sort."

Rox snapped out of her reverie and focused. It was Michael Serrano, standing just beside her, following the direction of her gaze.

"Okay," Michael said judiciously, "I'll admit that some of them *look* like steers, many have the intellectual acuity of steers, but you'll notice that steers walk on all fours and chew their cud, whereas these creatures have mostly learned to walk erect and chew tobacco."

Rox gave him the coldest look she had. "Go away. Don't talk to me. I still don't talk to rattlesnakes."

Michael Serrano was the only person in the school who fit neither into the locals category nor entirely into the Hollyweirdos category. Michael's family had moved to Montana from New York City.

Michael looked shocked. He slapped a hand over his heart. "Oh, you wound me, Rox. It's a whole new year. I can't believe you're still weighed down by the silly grudges and petty grievances of the past."

Rox curled her lip, a parody of the look the cheerleader Julia had given her. "Go away, Serrano. Nothing has changed. You're still like something I'd have to scrape off the bottom of my shoes."

He laughed, a genuine laugh of enjoyment. "I like that—'something I'd have to scrape off the bottom of my shoes.' Do you mind if I use that sometime?"

Rox stared at him. Her insult had had exactly zero effect. Michael was invulnerable to insult. It amazed her to think she had ever thought he was attractive, had even gone out with him once. Yes, he had all the outward signs of good looks—the cool green eyes, the excellent dark hair combed straight back off his forehead, the brilliant white smile. He even had a nice body. He was no Christopher, but in fairness, he was an attractive guy.

Until you got to know him.

"You know, it's true," Rox said. "It's a brand-new year. Let's start it off right. Let's agree right at the start that you won't speak to me."

She started to walk away.

"I understand," he said. "I really do. Your taste

in guys runs more toward dumb blond cowboy types who call you ma'am."

Rox knew she should just keep walking, but, foolishly, she turned back. "What are you talking about?"

"Please, like I don't know you've got it bad for Christopher MacAvoy? Like it somehow escaped my notice that he drove you here today? Like I didn't see that little smirk of triumph on your face when you skipped away from his truck, leaving the poor dumb crap-kicker blushing and aw-shucksing?" He stepped closer. "What did you do? How did you get him to drive you to school? Pull the old broken-down car routine?"

Rox blanched, and Michael grinned hugely, knowing instantly that he had guessed right.

"You're such a bastard, Serrano," Rox snapped. "You wouldn't understand."

"Oh, wouldn't I?" he said in a voice that nearly slithered. "And why exactly is it that you hate me so much? Let me see if I can remember. Was it an incident involving me running out of gas?"

"Running out of gas out on some godforsaken back road, miles from a gas station, but just a few yards from an abandoned cabin. An abandoned cabin that just *happened* to have a double bed, and where someone—who knows who?—had just *happened* to leave behind a bottle of chilled champagne, and the only light available *happened* to be candles."

"I grant you, it lacked subtlety," Michael admitted.

"I realize I overwrote the whole scene. But I was younger then. I'm a new man now. I've grown over the past year."

"Grown? You've just shed one skin for another," Rox shot back.

"You can deny it all you want, Rox Maslow," he said. "But you and I belong together. You really think you're going to make it with Christopher MacAvoy? He's the ultimate example of the locals. The guy rides bulls in the rodeo. He attends church. With his mother. He works. With his *hands*. Whereas, *you* . . ." He shook his head, mocking her. "Let's see, how much money does your father have? Would it be . . . more money than every other person in Montana put together? Almost. Not quite. I worked it out once with a calculator."

"Not everyone is as obsessed with money as you are, Serrano."

"Right. So it's going to be you and Cowboy Chris, huh? What do you think this is, Romeo and Juliet? In real life the Montagues and the Capulets don't get together. In real life it turns out that Romeo just wants a piece of the Maslow money like everyone else. You'll see."

"Christopher isn't like that," Rox said heatedly. "I don't expect you to understand, but he is decent and straightforward and good in a way you'll never be. Good. Do you even know that word? He's a good guy."

"That's just his act," Michael said.

31

"Oh, really? Then if he's so interested in my father's money, why won't he ask me out, even though I've practically thrown myself at him?"

Instantly Rox knew she had said too much. She could tell by the look of glee in Michael's eyes.

"Well, well," he drawled. "The things you can learn, even on the first day of school.

"You know, Rox," he said as he turned to leave, "it would almost serve you right if you did get something going with Christopher MacAvoy. The reality never lives up to the fantasy, and no one—I mean, *no one*—is as wholesome and decent as you think he is."

Christopher watched as green beans were piled on his tray and said, "Thank you, ma'am" to the green bean lady. Then he watched as a gelatinous Salisbury steak was plopped more or less on top of his mashed potatoes and said, "Thank you, ma'am" to the cafeteria lady who had done that. He said "thank you" again when he was handed his tray.

He became aware of someone staring at him. He turned slowly. The guy behind him in line, the one staring at him and shaking his head in disbelief, was a person Christopher recognized—there were only seventy-some people in the senior class—but not someone he could say he knew.

"You're very polite, aren't you?" Michael asked him.

Christopher shrugged. "Never really thought

about it," he said. He nodded—politely—and turned away, moving ahead with the line.

"We've never really met, have we?" Michael asked. "I mean, beyond knowing each other's names." He stuck out his hand. "I think it's time to remedy that."

Christopher hesitated a moment before shaking Michael's hand. His daddy had always said you could tell a lot about a person by his handshake. Michael's handshake was surprisingly firm. His palms were soft, like most of these new people, but it wasn't some limp, dead fish handshake.

"Glad to meet you," Christopher said. And having nothing else much to say, he started to turn away again.

"I believe we have a friend in common," Michael said.

Christopher got his carton of milk and paid for an extra one as well. "Could be."

"I was thinking of Rox Maslow," Michael said.

Christopher felt his heart trip. And then, as if in sympathy, his feet tripped, one boot tangling with the other. With both hands on his tray he nearly fell forward. But Michael's hand shot out, grabbed his elbow, and helped steady him.

"Thanks," Christopher said. He laughed, feeling a little foolish.

"I can see why Rox would have an effect on you," Michael said, grinning good-naturedly. "She's a very beautiful girl."

"I reckon she is," Christopher agreed softly.

"She and I used to be close," Michael said. "But I guess we were just too much alike to get along together. She's the kind of girl who likes a guy who's a little different. Someone who will *contrast* with her."

Christopher set his tray on one of the four-person tables and took a seat. Michael sat across from him. It was the kind of thing that would cause some people to take notice, not that Christopher paid any attention to what people thought of him. He shared the general dislike for the Hollyweirdos, but he had always refused to believe that they were *all* bad. Especially Rox. And if she could be from California and still be an angel, then why not Michael?

Of course he was actually from New York. . . . Still, only a fool would judge a guy before he even got to know him.

Christopher nodded a cordial hello to Julia Ardmore, who had taken a seat at the next table, just behind Michael. Christopher had gone out with Julia for a while, but his interest in her, never strong, had evaporated upon Rox's arrival. And in truth Julia had never seemed all that enamored of him, either.

When Michael did not seem inclined to say anything more on the subject of Rox Maslow, Christopher said, "Well, she seems like a nice person."

"Who?" Michael asked, wrinkling his brow quizzically.

"Rox Maslow," Christopher said.

"Oh, right. I'd forgotten we were even talking about her. Yeah, she is a nice person. Smart, sweet, generous, kind . . . affectionate." He lingered on that last word. Then he shrugged. "But, like I said, we didn't hit it off."

Christopher nodded, trying to control his desire to press for details. It wasn't really right to be talking about Rox with some guy he barely knew. It was close to gossip. But information about Rox was precious to him. Just the chance to say her name out loud was precious.

"Yeah?" Christopher said at last, when it was clear that Michael was losing interest again.

"Uh-huh," Michael said, chewing a bite of the Salisbury steak and looking slightly sick. "Yeah, she's a sweetheart. But the thing was, let's face it, I'm not exactly a real Montana kind of guy."

Christopher grinned and looked down at his plate, so as not to offend his new acquaintance.

"It's okay," Michael said with a self-deprecating laugh. "I *know* I'm not a cowboy. I was born and raised in the city. New York. Subways and skyscrapers, dirty air and dirty streets, crime. . . . Every day I'd walk to school and have to step over the body of some guy who'd been stabbed or shot. It was hell. Thank God I'm out of there." He shuddered. "But, anyway, Rox . . . she's in love with the whole Montana thing. The big sky, the mountains, the trout streams, the people . . . especially the people. She always used to talk about how different you folks are. Honest and decent and straightforward.

Hardworking and all. That was very attractive to her."

Christopher listened avidly. Of course Michael was exaggerating—the stuff about dead bodies in the streets—but he sensed a core of truth there, as well as in the part about Rox loving Montana. Or maybe he was just fooling himself. Maybe he was just believing what he wanted to believe.

"She shouldn't hold it against you that you're from New York City," Christopher said generously. "I'll bet you're just as hardworking and honest and . . . all that other stuff. I imagine folks are pretty much the same everywhere."

"Absolutely," Michael said. "Greenwich Village, Longhorn, Montana, same-o, same-o. So, anyway, why all the questions about Rox?" He winked. "You like her, huh?"

Christopher was taken aback. Had he been too obvious? "I've only just spoken to her twice."

"Well, she's a girl that loves a good conversation. You know, like we're having right now, the two of us. It was the one thing we had in common—we both enjoyed talking. She can stay up all night talking about her plans, or the way the world is, or sometimes just reading aloud from a book of poetry and discussing it. Talk, talk, talk." A sly look lit his eyes and then vanished. "You should ask her out."

Christopher sighed miserably. "I don't know about that."

"Why not? I would think she'd really fall for a guy like you. You lucky dog."

Christopher looked around to see if anyone was listening in. "See, the thing is, I'm not much good at talking."

"What do you mean? You're talking to me, aren't you?"

"That's different. See . . . you're another fellow. I can talk to another fellow. I can talk to some of these girls I've grown up with. Mostly, anyway. But whenever I even think about trying to talk to Rox . . . everything just flies out of my head, and my mouth won't work, and I end up looking like a jackass. Not a very smart jackass, either."

"Hmm. Boy, that is a problem," Michael said, nodding thoughtfully. "Of course, with a little practice you could probably get over it in time."

"You can't practice if you can't even start," Christopher said, laughing ruefully.

"True," Michael agreed. And then the sly light came on again in his green eyes. For a moment his entire face glowed, as if he had received a revelation. "You know," he said, "maybe what you need is a little tutoring. Tutoring in the fine art of conversation." He grinned. "A *love* tutor, you might say."

Christopher shrugged. "Where would I find a love tutor?"

Chapter Four

"Now, as you know, the work-study pro-gram is a for-credit opportunity for you to combine your academic studies with an opportunity to earn some money," the teacher, Mrs. Lyme, said. "Participation is not mandatory, however. Some of you don't need the class credit. And some of you don't need the money."

The teacher did not direct the remark at Rox in particular, or even look at her. But several of the other students in the class did.

"In any event, there is a list, posted up here on the board, of establishments that have openings."

Off to one side of the room, Rox saw Michael Serrano's hand go up. "I hope some of those coveted Dairy Queen jobs will be available," he said. "I'll need ice-cream cone dipping skills if I hope to compete in the global marketplace of tomorrow."

"Actually, most of the jobs are with A.T.C. Services," Mrs. Lyme said. "They answer 800-number lines for people like those television cable shopping stations. A chance to earn money just by moving your mouth. Should be right up your alley, Michael."

Her remark earned a laugh from the class, including Rox.

Someone tapped Rox's shoulder. A folded piece of notebook paper appeared. Rox reached back discreetly to take it. She unfolded it and read the message. *I saw you in C's truck this morning. What happened? D.*

Darby Todd. She was seated two rows back.

While the teacher droned on, Rox tore a sheet of paper from her binder. *My car had a flat tire. He drove me to school, that's all. R.*

A minute later the response arrived from Darby. *Yeah, right. I want details, girl. D.*

But the bell rang before Rox could decide what details to give. She met up with Darby in the hallway.

Darby's parents managed the Pecos Pete Ranch for Rox's father, tolerating his odd ideas and keeping the place from devolving into complete anarchy. They lived in a separate residence on a far corner of the ranch.

At first things had been a little uncertain between Rox and Darby. After all, Darby's father worked for Rox's father, and Darby was determined not to be treated like a hired hand by Rox, who she

40

assumed was another snooty Hollywood kid with too much money and no sense.

As it happened, none of the Todds were ever treated like hired hands. In fact, after the incident of the freezing ostriches, the Todds pretty much took over the running of the ranch and treated Craig Maslow like a slightly crazy relative—someone to whom you had to be polite but didn't have to pay too much attention.

Darby and Rox had hit it off almost from the start. Rox had asked Darby for help in selecting Drifter and in learning to ride Western style; Darby had asked Rox to get her in to meet Ethan Hawke when he'd visited the ranch for a day to discuss a project with Rox's father. Rox had been totally happy with Drifter, Darby had shaken hands with Ethan Hawke, and the friendship was firmly established.

"Okay, quick," Darby said. "I have history next and old Schwegel freaks if you're even eight seconds late. What happened with you and Christopher?"

"I had a flat tire, so he picked me up."

"And . . . ?"

"And nothing much," Rox admitted.

"Let me guess. He said 'uh' and 'um' and 'yes, ma'am' a lot," Darby said.

"And gulping. Don't forget the nervous gulping thing," Rox said crossly.

Darby sighed. "That doesn't necessarily mean he doesn't like you. Did you see him talking to Michael at lunch?"

"Who?" Rox practically shouted. She clutched at Darby's arm. "Serrano? Christopher was talking to Michael Serrano at lunch?"

"What's the big deal?" Darby shook off Rox's grip. "I figured he was talking to Michael because he thinks Michael knows you. You know, Christopher was probably trying to find out from Michael if you like him."

"I don't want Christopher finding out about me from Michael. Michael is not the expert on me. Michael is the expert on summoning demons from the fiery pit and selling his shriveled little soul to them," Rox said.

"I think he's kind of cute," Darby said, deliberately provoking Rox.

"Christopher having lunch with Michael." Rox shook her head. "It's like seeing Gandhi hanging out with Hitler. Good and evil brought together over Salisbury steak." She shuddered. She had reason to worry about Christopher talking to Michael. Michael had guessed the truth about the "flat" tire.

"Look, relax. Christopher is a little shy. He was probably just pumping Michael for information."

Exactly what I'm worried about, Rox thought.

"Maybe you should try the same kind of thing," Darby suggested.

"What kind of thing?"

"You know, get some inside information from someone who knows Christopher."

"*You* know Christopher, and all you can tell me

42

is that he's shy, which I kind of figured out all on my own."

"Yeah, but how about some of the girls he's gone out with?"

Rox stopped dead. "He's gone out?"

Darby made a face. "Of course. He's not a monk. He used to kind of go with Tricia in tenth grade. And last summer—right before you got here—he was going with Julia. They broke up soon after school started, though. You know Julia, right? Really thin, very cute, long reddish brown hair?"

"Of course I know Julia," Rox snapped. "When I ran for student council, she's the one who arranged for the ballot to read 'Rot Maslow.' Don't tell me she didn't; I know she did."

"Well, setting aside your paranoid delusions . . . Julia and Christopher were a thing for a while. Maybe you should try and get some insight from her."

Rox laughed. "Yeah, right. Julia Ardmore. That would be just perfect. I should go to a girl who hates me to get information on how to get together with a guy she broke up with who, it seems, is getting information about me from a guy I despise."

Darby laughed. "Getting the senior year off to a fast start, aren't you?"

"Rox, I realize we haven't known each other long and yet I have the feeling that we are destined to know each other much better. Maybe I'm just being a hopeless romantic, but dot dot dot anyway,

43

I guess what I'm trying to say is, would you do me the honor of accompanying me to the dance this Friday?" Christopher exhaled sharply. "There. I got through it."

Christopher was leaning against the front fender of his pickup in the rapidly emptying school parking lot. Michael was sitting cross-legged on the hood of someone's car, not his own, looking like a Buddha.

There was some shade in the parking lot—huge old willows that had been saplings back when the school was built in 1889. The school building was two stories, brick and stone, impressive looking if you didn't look long enough to realize how small it was. Off to the side the football team was running laps around the athletic field. The cheerleaders were having tryouts to replace the girls who had graduated the year before.

Michael stared at Christopher with a look of amused pity and shook his head. "You're really not very good at this, are you, Christopher?"

"What's the matter?"

"'Dot dot dot'? What is 'dot dot dot'?"

"That's what you said to say," Christopher said, a little alarmed.

"Christopher, I meant like an ellipsis. You know, the three dots at the end of a phrase? So it sounds like you're just letting the sentence hang in midair? That's what I meant. 'Maybe I'm just being a hopeless romantic, but,' pause, ellipsis, let it hang for a second."

"Why?"

"Because there's nothing else you can *say* at that point. You want to just *imply*. See, what can you say after, 'Maybe I'm just a hopeless romantic, but'? 'Maybe I'm just a hopeless romantic, but I see a future with the two of us sharing a mobile home parked next to my mom's farmhouse, filled with squalling brats and unpaid bills, because your dad has cut you off in horror at the fact that you've married a clod-kicker cowboy'?"

Christopher looked closely at Michael. Yes, Michael *was* making fun of him. There was no doubt on that point. Then again, maybe this was just good-natured joshing. Put another way, it had *better* be good-natured joshing.

Michael smiled and winked to show he was just kidding.

Christopher nodded guardedly and relaxed. Some of these city people had different ways of saying things, more "in-your-face" than would be thought polite around here. But that didn't mean it was malicious. He would give Michael the benefit of the doubt—for now.

"Try it again," Michael prompted.

Christopher struck a pose. "Rox," he announced to no one, "I realize we haven't known each other long and yet I have the feeling that we are destined to know each other much better. Maybe I'm just being a hopeless romantic, but . . . anyway, I guess what I'm trying to say is, would you do me the honor of accompanying me to the dance this Friday?"

"Perfect. See? It's easy. Nothing to it. You just

need to build up your confidence a little," Michael said soothingly. "That's all it is, confidence."

Christopher shook his head dubiously. "It's a lot easier with you than it will be with Rox," he said. "I mean, I'm not looking at you thinking I'd really like to—"

"You'd better not be," Michael interrupted.

"—hold your hand."

Michael's expression was almost pained. "Hold hands? *That's* what you want to do with Rox Maslow? Hold hands? Huh. Does she *have* hands? I've never looked that far to the side before," Michael said.

"I'd like to hold her hand, yes, I would," Christopher said softly. "That would be fine, to hold her hand and maybe look up at the moon for a while."

"You know, Christopher, it's easier and quicker getting that big home run if you start on first base and not in the dugout," Michael said, emphasizing his point by wiggling his eyebrows.

"Home run?" Christopher felt the blood rising in him. "I do appreciate all the help you're giving me, Michael," he said in a dangerous, low voice. "But there won't be any talk like that about Rox. She's a lady. And she'll be treated like a lady."

"Yes, she *is* a lady," Michael agreed quickly. "I apologize if I sounded disrespectful."

"No harm done," Christopher allowed generously.

"Anyway, look, all you have to do is say to her

what we worked out here, and I think she'll go to that dance with you."

Christopher kneaded the back of his neck with one hand. "Just thinking about it I'm getting tight." He looked around and suddenly saw her. She was a hundred yards away, just coming out of the front door of the school with Darby Todd.

Would she come over and ask Christopher for a ride home? He hoped so—fervently. And hoped not—just as fervently. He was nowhere near ready to be alone with her for the whole long drive. The little speech he'd memorized would only fill about ten seconds. Maybe twenty, if he kept screwing it up.

He felt a wave of hopelessness, made all the more powerful by the almost sickening wave of longing that came immediately behind it. Rox was laughing, sharing some joke with Darby. In the slanting rays of the afternoon sun her skin glowed pink. He could imagine her at the dance, in the sort of dress she would wear to a dance—black, or red, maybe, with one of those low necklines, and probably kind of short, and maybe even with high-heeled shoes. She was so elegant, so far above anyone a simple person like Christopher MacAvoy should ever have on his arm.

"I think maybe I better just forget about this," Christopher said.

Michael followed the direction of his gaze. "I'm surprised to hear you say that," he said. "I would never have guessed you were any kind of coward."

Christopher turned an angry stare on Michael.

47

But then, just as quickly as it had shown up, Christopher's dark mood vanished. "I get it," he said. "You're trying to provoke me into sticking with it. Well, you're right. I don't believe I am a coward."

"Then let's try it one more time," Michael prodded.

"Okay. One more time. Rox, I realize we haven't known each other long and yet I have the feeling that we are destined to know each other much better. Maybe I'm just being a hopeless romantic, but dot dot dot. Dang!"

"Yeah, you want to watch that," Michael said dryly.

"I've got those dots stuck in my head now. Okay. Maybe I'm just hopeless—I mean, maybe I'm just being a hopeless romantic, but . . . anyway, I guess what I'm trying to say is, would you do me the honor of accompanying me to the dance this Friday?"

"Perfect," Michael said.

"I'm grateful for your helping me like this," Christopher said. "If I can ever repay you, just say the word."

"Just seeing you two get together will be all the payment I need," Michael said, clapping a friendly hand on Christopher's shoulder. "I feel like I can consider you a friend now, and that's a nice feeling."

"I reckon it is," Christopher agreed. It seemed a little quick to be throwing around a word like 'friend,' but Michael was certainly acting like a friend.

48

"I have to confess . . . it has been a little lonely being so isolated from guys like you at school," Michael said, revealing just the beginning of an emotional quaver in his voice.

The sentiment made Christopher very uncomfortable. "Well, now it doesn't even look like I'll get a chance to try out the speech," he said. "At least not right away." He pointed toward a white Range Rover emblazoned with the colorful logo—you couldn't exactly call it a brand, when it included a cartoon character—of the Pecos Pete Ranch. The Range Rover pulled to a stop on the street in front of the school. Rox gave Darby a quick good-bye kiss on the cheek and ran down to the Range Rover. Then, to Christopher's profound joy, she hesitated with the vehicle's door open, turned, spotted him, and gave a little wave and a smile.

"Wave back to her, for God's sake!" Michael hissed.

Christopher did, belatedly, but by then Rox was inside the Range Rover. Whether she'd seen him or not, he couldn't tell.

"This romance thing is really not one of your basic skills, is it, Christopher?" Michael asked, sounding amused and a little discouraged.

"No. It sure isn't. I'll try and learn this one speech you've taught me, though. Maybe that'll at least get me started. I'm indebted to you," he said, looking Michael in the eye. "And I always pay my debts. But . . ."

"But what?"

49

"Well, I would appreciate if you wouldn't take the Lord's name in vain."

Michael threw up his hands. "Good . . . I mean, for . . ." He sighed. "For crying out loud."

"Thanks," Christopher said. He clapped his hand on Michael's shoulder. "I guess you think it's foolish to object to a thing like that."

"No, no," Michael said quickly. "When in Rome, do as the Romans do." Then he laughed, a short, genuinely bitter sound. "You know, it's about nineteen hundred miles back to New York," he said thoughtfully. "Sometimes I think maybe I should just walk."

"No need to walk," Christopher said, deadpan. "There's plenty of folks around here who would chip in for bus fare. Not me, though. Not anymore. You're all right by me."

Chapter Five

Rox's room was actually two rooms, not counting her own private bathroom. There was the main bedroom, with a ceiling that sloped low in the corner and rose to a height of fifteen feet by the time it met the far wall. The ceiling was made of closely joined logs. The walls were knotty pine, the floors polished cedar, mostly covered with ornate Southwestern-theme rugs.

The room was in the same rustic style as the entire house, where wood was pretty much the design theme. Wood and tall windows, and wood and extravagant extrusions of twisted metal that were supposed to be sculptures, and more wood, and huge canvases painted by some of the finest artists of the last fifty years, and more wood.

Rox had managed to preserve her own rooms from the strange mix of ultramodern art and extreme rusticity that her father had dictated. But there wasn't anything she could do about the wood. Which was fine, because she liked the wood, even though it made hanging posters a little awkward.

Off her main bedroom she had a study room where she had her desk and state-of-the-art computer and a well-stocked reference library of books, CDs, and videos. She had a balcony off the study room where she had set up a tripod for her telescope, and on clear, cool nights she went out and looked at the stars and the moons of Jupiter.

Her bathroom was more wood, more log walls and sloping roofs, and more floor-to-ceiling windows. Even the Jacuzzi bath was raised on a platform made of hewn logs. The facilities, of course, were all completely modern, including the stereo speakers in every room and the television screens that were positioned before her bed, beside her desk, and over the Jacuzzi. The house had a system that allowed her, using a remote control panel, to call up any of 150 movies (including all her father's movies) at any time.

Rox had three phones, one in each room.

And as she sat in the center of her gigantic California king-size bed and leafed distractedly through a *Mademoiselle,* none of the three phones was ringing.

Christopher's room was small, with somewhat low ceilings and two square windows, one overlooking the front yard, the other looking out at the big silver-painted propane tank.

The walls were painted white and were decorated with rodeo posters, one showing a beautiful shot of a huge Brahma bull completely airborne, all four legs in the air, with a cowboy on his back, hand thrown back, hat flying free, a fierce grin on his face.

He had a tiny desk stuck under the front window, piled with schoolbooks and an aging IBM clone. His hat was hung on the back of the chair. There was a small round nightstand beside his bed, just big enough for his clock radio, keys, and watch.

He sat on a single bed, on a faded quilt his grandmother had made for his parents' wedding. He had carried the telephone in from the hallway. Beside it he had a small spiral notebook, open to a page that had a single name and a single phone number. He was staring at the telephone and at the telephone number.

"Rox," he muttered under his breath, "I realize we haven't known each other long and yet I have the feeling that we are destined to know each other much better. Maybe I'm just being a hopeless romantic, but . . . anyway, I guess what I'm trying to say is, would you do me the honor of accompanying me to the dance this Friday?"

He reached for the phone, but stopped. He wiped his palms on his jeans. His hands were sweaty. His heart was hammering like a drummer who'd had one too many cups of coffee.

"You *are* going to call her," he ordered himself sternly. What kind of a coward wouldn't even call a girl on the phone? What kind of a man was he if he was terrified of a girl? No kind of man, that was the answer. He was no kind of a man unless he made this call.

He looked up at the picture of the cowboy on the bull. The cowboy was Tuff Hedeman. He had broken his neck bull riding. And even though he'd already won every title he could win and had nothing left to prove to anyone, he'd still gone back to bull riding. Once he'd recovered the use of his limbs. Now *that* was a man. He never was afraid of anything, let alone calling a girl on the telephone.

But the truth was, Christopher would infinitely rather face the biggest, meanest bull ever birthed than to make this call. A bull could only kill you, and that didn't happen often. Mostly it would just give you some good bruises, or maybe break a couple of ribs. Or give you a swift butt in the butt. He rubbed the spot where his own behind was still sore.

"Rox," he muttered under his breath, "I realize we haven't known each other long and yet I have the feeling that we are destined to know each other much better. Maybe I'm just being a hopeless romantic, but dot dot dot . . . *No!* No dots. Stop the dots! Forget the dots."

There was an article in *Mademoiselle* called "Making the First Move." It listed ten ways for a girl to ask a guy out. Ten ways, and none of them involved deliberately letting the air out of your tires and tricking the guy into giving you a ride. Rox felt bad about that. The truth was it was underhanded, and that bothered Rox. It was such a sleazy, manipulative, *California* kind of thing to do. It was definitely not Montana.

How could she hope to get together with Christopher using underhanded California tricks? It was missing the whole point. The very thing that attracted her to Christopher was the fact that he was so open and honest and decent. And here she was, laying sneaky traps for him.

She ought to just call him. That would be the Montana way—forthright, straight up, direct.

Only . . . wasn't the very idea of a girl calling a guy kind of a California sort of thing? Wouldn't he be appalled if she called him?

Not as appalled as he would be if he ever found out about the tire.

How had Julia Ardmore ever gone out with Christopher? Granted, she had known him all her life, but still, someone had made the first move. Had Christopher just called her up and asked her out? If so, then why on earth couldn't he do it now?

She stared malevolently at the nearest phone. "Because he doesn't like you," Rox said. "Figure it out, girl—he doesn't like you. If he liked you, he'd call, wouldn't he?"

Why? Why was it always up to the guy to make the first move? Christopher asked himself. It was

55

wrong. This was the nineties, girls could call guys, couldn't they? He'd been in the IGA the other day and seen one of those girls' magazines with a story on the cover, something about ways for the girl to make the first move.

Why couldn't Rox just get that magazine and then call him? She would know what to say. It would be so *easy* for her. All she had to do was call and say, "Hey, Christopher, I was wondering if you'd like to go to the dance on Friday?" And then all he would have to say was, "Yes, I would like that fine."

He could manage that. Yes, that was clearly the way it should go. She should call *him*. And then he wouldn't have to call her. And then he wouldn't have to feel like such a hopeless, gutless, cowardly—

He snatched up the phone, suddenly decisive. He dialed the numbers—555-0765.

There. The call was being switched. The phone was ringing. Her phone. Her phone was ringing, and that meant she would pick it up and then he would have to—

The ringing made Rox jump. The magazine flew out of her hand.

"Chill!" she ordered herself. "Good grief, Rox, it's probably just Darby."

She took a deep breath. A second ring. Wait till the third ring or it would seem like she'd just been sitting there, waiting. It rang again.

Rox snatched up the phone.

"Hello?"

56

There was no answer. Then the phone clicked, and the line went dead.

Michael Serrano's room was, as much as he could help it, not even *in* Montana. The walls were painted a subtle light matte gray, not too bright, not too dark. The room had track lighting and a wavy strip of blue neon that swirled down one wall.

The full-size bed was covered with a black-and-gray geometric print spread. The walls were decorated with professionally mounted posters—one of Trent Reznor, and a huge blowup photograph of midtown Manhattan from the air. There was a bulletin board covered with black-and-white still photos of various Hollywood people. Not actors, for the most part. These were photos of deal makers and power brokers—Steven Spielberg, Michael Ovitz, Jeffrey Katzenberg, Michael Eisner, and, most prominently, right in the center, Craig Maslow.

And then there was the framed poster advertising last year's Longhorn Film Festival. The event was sponsored by Maslow and attended by half the movie stars, directors, and producers in Hollywood. Michael had moved heaven and earth to find a way inside that film festival. He had been caught dressing as a waiter and had been threatened with arrest if he came back.

This year's festival was only twelve days away. He was thinking of trying to pass himself off as a florist delivering a bouquet to some lucky producer. A bouquet that might just have a copy of his not entirely finished screenplay stuck inside.

Michael had a large desk, a glass slab resting on two stainless steel pillars. It held a computer whose screen saver was a rotating, fading, flying dollar bill. The computer was connected to CompuServe, Prodigy, America Online, and any other service that would let Michael connect with people outside Montana.

In an upturned stationery box sat a hundred pages or so, representing the latest incarnation of the screenplay Michael had been working on for a year—ever since Craig Maslow had relocated more or less permanently to Montana.

The screenplay was titled *Escape!* It was the story of a sophisticated, intelligent teenage boy who is forced against his will (very much against his will) to relocate from New York to a small town in Wyoming. But the boy in question has wit and irresistible good looks, and he is able to romance the daughter of a famous and powerful TV producer. This producer immediately realizes that his daughter's boyfriend is much more than he seemed at first, and he gives the guy a role on his hit TV series.

It was deliberately *not* autobiographical, because Michael had read once that being too autobiographical in writing a screenplay was considered amateurish. So Wyoming had taken the place of Montana, and a TV producer had taken the place of Craig Maslow, who was, after all, more of a movie producer and director.

He would have gladly traded anything he had for the chance to sneak that screenplay into the film festival and the hands of a man like Maslow. But, by the same token, the security guys might not be so tolerant a second time.

Michael's phone was resting atop the screenplay sheets, keeping the pages in place. It rang, and Michael went to pick it up.

"Yeah?"

"Hi. This is Christopher MacAvoy; is this Michael Serrano?"

"Yeah, Christopher, it's me. What's up, man?" Michael grinned, anticipating the response.

"Um, look here, the thing is, I was just getting ready to call a certain person—"

"Rox."

"Yep. I was just fixing to call her up and say the words we were practicing this afternoon. And the thing was, I had it all ready, all loaded up and ready to go, only when I actually heard her say hello . . . I kind of like went blank."

Michael covered the mouthpiece with his hand and held the receiver out to stare at it. "You are so totally pathetic, you hopeless dweeb of a crap-kicking cowboy. If you were any dumber, it'd be the cows branding you, instead of the other way around," he murmured almost silently. Then he put the receiver back to his ear. "Well, that's normal, I guess, Christopher," Michael said in a smooth, concerned voice. "It's perfectly normal to be a little nervous."

"I nearly threw up afterward. I was more than a little nervous."

Michael had to laugh. "That *is* nervous."

"Yeah, I guess if it was the other way around, I'd be laughing, too," Christopher said ruefully. "The thing is, now I can't remember any of it. Except 'dot dot dot.' *That* I can still remember."

"Hmm," Michael said.

"Yeah," Christopher said.

"This may be more difficult than I thought at first."

"I won't impose on you anymore," Christopher said. "If you could only just remind me of what it was."

Michael rolled his eyes. This really shouldn't be all that difficult. Christopher was hot for Rox. Rox was hot for Christopher. And yet if he, Michael, didn't take a hand in this, the whole matter could drag on inconclusively for the rest of the year. And that would not do.

No, that would not do at all. These two kids had to get together. Because only then could they be ripped apart.

Only then would Michael's brilliant plan work.

"Christopher, my friend," Michael said, "I think we're going to have to take more complete measures here. As you've probably guessed, I'm a bit of a romantic myself. And I just think true love should never be allowed to fail. Certainly not for lack of a few well-chosen words."

He heard Christopher sigh, a discouraged sound.

"Hey, don't give up, man," Michael said. "This is going to work, don't you worry. Listen, do you happen to own a computer?"

"A computer? Yes, I have one. It's kind of old."

"That's okay," Michael said. "Don't worry about a thing. Are you hooked up to any on-line services?"

"We have CompuServe," Christopher said, still mystified.

"Good enough. You have two phone lines?"

"Sure do. One for the business."

"Cool. Then we are *in* business. Turn on your computer, boy. We are going to do some high-tech seduction."

"Seduction?" Christopher clearly did not like the word.

"Courting? Is that a better word?"

"Courting. Yes, that's a fine word. A little old-fashioned, maybe, but it gets the point across."

Ten minutes later Christopher typed the words *Michael. Are you here?* on his computer keyboard. The words he'd just typed appeared on the screen.

Seconds later the words *I'm right here, cowboy, let's do it* appeared on Christopher's computer screen.

The connection had been made.

Chapter Six

ROX HAD BECK on the stereo as she waited in her bathrobe for the Jacuzzi to fill. Between the noise Beck was making and the noise of the rushing water, she almost didn't hear her phone ring.

But the electronic trilling finally cut through the background noise. She picked up the receiver absentmindedly. She had long since given up on the idea that Christopher might call. It was after nine, and she knew that ranch kids kept very early hours.

"Yes?" she said in a loud voice.

"Um, uh, h-h-h-hi. Hi. I mean, hello. Howdy."

"What?" Rox looked around for the remote to turn down the music.

"Is is is is is is this um . . . is this . . . are you Roxana? Maslow? Roxana Maslow? Are you? Ma'am?"

Rox found the remote and muted the music. There was something familiar about the voice, but it was still a bit alarming. The person on the other end of the line was stammering, and sounded like he was choking on a piece of food.

Christopher! Of course.

"Yes, this is Rox," she said eagerly. "Is that you, Christopher?"

"Um . . . is it? Yes, it's me."

"I'm glad you called," Rox said warmly. She sat on the bed and crossed her legs.

"Um . . . the thing I wanted to say was . . . Um, Rox? I um, realize we haven't known each other long and yet I have the feeling that we are destined to, you know, to, um, to to to . . . to know each other much better."

His voice was stiff and stilted, almost as if he were reading a speech, but it was the words Rox listened to.

"Maybe I'm, um, just hopeless. . . . I mean, maybe I'm a hopeless romantic, but . . . pause . . . I mean, no, I didn't mean to say 'pause.' Anyway, I guess what I'm trying to say is, wouldyoudomethe-honor of accompanying me? To the dance? This Friday?"

Rox heard him exhale heavily, as if he had just been bench-pressing a tractor. She smiled. She would never in a million years have guessed that Christopher was capable of saying such a very sweet thing.

"If you don't want to, well—"

"No," she said quickly, "I'd be happy to go to the dance with you Friday."

She heard a sharp intake of breath, followed by what sounded vaguely like someone typing on a keyboard.

"You would?" Christopher said. "I mean . . . I mean . . . um, what I mean is, thank you. Thank you for . . . for letting my heart beat again, Rox. I feel as if the sun and the moon and the stars are all in the sky at once, and each of them is you."

Rox pressed a hand over her heart. She'd never heard anything so romantic before. And certainly no one had ever said anything remotely so romantic to *her*. She was a little stunned. "Wow," she said at last. "I don't know what to say."

There was a pause, and again Rox had the sense that she could hear someone typing. Then Christopher said, "By saying 'yes,' you've already said more than I had any right to expect. I don't know how I'll ever sleep, thinking of Friday. And yet I'll have to sleep—how else could I dream of you?"

"Wow," Rox said again. "Are you sure this is Christopher MacAvoy?"

She had meant it as a little joke, but his voice was suddenly alarmed.

"What do you mean?"

"I just meant . . . I mean, this morning, and the other day, you've never had much to say to me."

"I do apologize for that. I . . ." There was another pause. Stiffly he said, "When I am actually in your presence, I am too awed to express myself well."

"Odd? You're too odd? Wait, I'm sorry. You mean awed, right? As in impressed?"

"Yes, that's what I meant."

"I think maybe you're just a little shy," Rox said gently. "But you know what? I'm loud enough for the both of us. I'm awfully glad you called."

"Me too," he said. "Only . . . if we meet at school tomorrow, and I pray we will, don't think badly of me if I cannot give voice to all I feel for you."

Rox laughed. "In other words, you'll still be awed?"

Christopher laughed, too, a nice sound, like pebbles in a rushing stream. And in his more usual laconic tone he said, "Awed and odd, too, I reckon."

Christopher hung up the phone and saw that his hand was shaking. His brow was beaded with sweat, although the room was not warm.

He looked at his computer screen. The last message from Michael was still there. *If we meet at school tomorrow, and I pray we will, don't think badly of me if I cannot give voice to all I feel for you.*

A new message appeared: *So?*

Christopher wiped the sweat off his forehead with his sleeve. He set his fingers over the keys and typed. His own message appeared on the screen just below the word *So.*

It's over. It worked! At the end she said would I still be awed when I saw her. I said I reckoned I'd be awed and odd, too. Was that all right?

Christopher waited a few seconds as Michael's words, being typed just a few miles away in town, raced along the phone lines all the way to Ohio, where they were handled and directed by the CompuServe computers, shunted into the chat room, and picked up by Christopher, all the way back in Montana.

Michael wrote, *Yeah, no harm done, I guess. But don't ad-lib, too much, okay?*

I'm grateful for the help, Christopher wrote. *I guess I can take it from here.*

Sure you can, Christopher. No prob.

Christopher turned off his computer. He felt at once excited and scared and filled with some new, unfamiliar sensation. It was a vague discomfort, a squirmy, unsettling feeling. It was as if somewhere, deep down, an alarm bell were ringing. A feeling that he couldn't really pin down, much the way he would just get a "feel" when one of the animals was sick, even though there was no outward sign, and then have no way of explaining how he'd known something was wrong.

"I know what it is," he muttered under his breath. "It's knowing that now I have a real date with Rox, and I don't know how I'll get through it."

That sounded plausible. That must be it. That had to be why he had this bad feeling. And yet it wasn't.

"Yeah, right, Chris, old boy," Michael said contemptuously. "Sure, you can handle it from here.

67

Ha! By tomorrow you'll be in a cold sweat, worrying about the big date."

Michael did not turn his computer off immediately. Instead he checked to see that he had properly recorded the entire exchange between himself and Christopher. It was there—misspellings and all. It was a simple matter for him to print the transcript.

The printer emitted only a low whir as it printed out the three pages.

Proof. Proof that he could use when the time was right.

He caught sight of himself in the full-length mirror that hung on his closet door. He smiled at his reflection.

"Nyah hah hah HAH!" he laughed, a high-pitched, vaguely disturbing laugh.

"That was good," he said, pleased with his own rendition of an evil laugh. "See? Why shouldn't I *act* as well as write, direct, and produce? Michael Serrano—the man who does it all in Hollywood."

Michael took the pages, straightened them, and slid them underneath the pages of his screenplay. He stepped closer to the mirror to frame a better close-up of his face.

In an announcer's voice he said, "While Serrano originally began his career in Hollywood as a protégé of Craig Maslow, his talents soon . . . his amazing array of talents . . . soon enabled him to completely overshadow the older man. Writer, actor, director, producer, and *People* magazine's

Sexiest Man Alive, Michael Serrano. And two-time Oscar winner. Maybe three, depending."

He glanced at the pile of homework on a corner of his desk. Not worth bothering with tonight, he thought. He could easily take care of it in the morning while eating breakfast. Schoolwork had never been a problem for him. He was, after all, a genius.

He winked at the mirror image of himself. "Nyah hah hah, YES!" He thrust his hand, fingers spread and pointing up, straight toward the ceiling.

Yes, that was an even better evil laugh. The hand gesture was great. He'd have to remember that.

Chapter Seven

B Y THE NEXT afternoon the heat wave had disappeared, replaced by a pleasantly cool breeze blowing down the mountains. Rox rode Drifter at an easy canter alongside Darby, who was on her horse, Mickey. The clear sky, combined with the cooler weather, made them all, human and horse alike, feel frisky and energetic and optimistic.

Rox was still feeling a glow of pleasure from the phone call the night before, even though that day at school Christopher had treated her with the same panicked shyness as before. That had disappointed her just a bit, but, she reminded herself, it would probably take a while for him to loosen up. And she wasn't sure how loose he was ever likely to get.

In theory they were riding just to exercise the horses. But in reality Rox had a goal in mind, and when that goal came in sight, and when Darby, oblivious to the secret agenda, seemed to want to drift off in the wrong direction, Rox signaled Drifter and he broke into a gallop.

"Hey!" Darby yelled.

"Yah!" Rox yelled back over her shoulder. "Try and catch me."

"All right, girl!" Darby yelled. "You asked for it!"

Soon the two horses were at full speed, and both riders were urging their mounts on and giggling with the sheer, giddy excitement of speed. After a few hundred yards Darby caught up to Rox, and they both slowed their horses to a gentler trot.

"Where are you going?" Darby asked. "As if I couldn't guess."

"Nowhere," Rox said, not expecting her friend to believe her.

"You are such a liar," Darby said with a laugh. "You're heading us toward the Three Aces. You think *he's* waiting for you out by the pond again?"

"We're just going for a ride," Rox insisted smugly. "Does everything have to *mean* something?"

"Yes," Darby said flatly.

The line of the fence, now newly strung with wire, was just ahead. Rox eased Drifter into a walk, and Darby and Mickey followed.

"You know, back home in California the way you do this is a little different," Rox said. "See, if I were there, what I would do is drive by a guy's house and see if maybe he was out in his yard or something."

"Or swimming naked in his pond," Darby suggested dryly.

"I never should have told you about that," Rox said. She rose up in her stirrups to look ahead. What she saw was disappointing. There was no pickup truck anywhere in sight. And no horse tied off to any of the trees surrounding the pond. Why had she thought there might be? she wondered.

Darby had the same question. "What makes you think he'd be out here?"

Rox shrugged. "Nothing. It's just that . . . it's just that it would have been kind of romantic. You know, it would be like he *sensed* that I would look for him here at the pond, and like he knew I would *sense* that he'd be here, and we'd meet and it would be like fate or something."

"Right. Because Christopher MacAvoy is such a romantic."

They came to a stop by the fence, just up the hill from the pond. The horses snorted and panted. The girls just panted.

"He *is* romantic," Rox said. "I told you all the things he said on the phone. It was the most romantic phone call in my entire life. It was the most romantic phone call I've ever even heard about."

"I have to admit, it sounded that way," Darby said guardedly. "I'm just wondering if maybe you didn't exaggerate a little. You know, like it sounded cool and all because he was actually speaking in complete sentences."

"No, it was *not* just that he was speaking in

73

complete sentences. It was what he said. You're just jealous because no one is calling you and sounding poetic and romantic."

Darby laughed easily. "Maybe that's true."

"I'm *so* looking forward to this date with him."

Darby looked sharply at her. "You're scared, aren't you?"

Rox nodded. As usual her friend had seen right through her. "Yeah, a little, I guess. I mean, look, everyone at school, all the locals, anyway, think I'm the devil's own daughter. And Christopher is *so* local, if you know what I mean. Some of the people around here think I used to have Hollywood sex orgies where we'd all be snorting entire bowls of cocaine."

"You're saying that's not true?" Darby dead-panned.

"I was the same normal, boring person in California that I am here," Rox said. She leaned forward to stroke Drifter's neck.

"You're not *so* normal," Darby teased. "Boring, sure."

"You know what worries me," Rox said. "This dance. I mean, we hardly know each other, and as shy as he is face-to-face, I'm afraid he's just going to freeze up like Medusa when she saw her own reflection."

"Like what?"

"You know, Medusa with the snake head. Whenever anyone saw her, they turned to stone, so when she saw her own reflection—"

"Okay, okay. What you need to do is try and spend a little time with him under less intense circumstances. Why don't you just have lunch with him or something, you know? Just plop down at his table in the cafeteria."

Rox considered, then shook her head. "Too public. See, part of the problem is all the people looking at us. That kind of pressure, plus the fact that he seems to have a hard time expressing his feelings . . ."

"Okay. I got it—ride over to his house and ask him to go riding with you."

Rox thought Darby's suggestion over for a moment. "No, I can't just spring something on him suddenly. Last time I did that, I walked in on him in a state of pantslessness."

"And that was a *bad* thing, right?" Darby asked with a grin. "What you need is some normal, natural reason to get together with him. Ha, I got it! The perfect solution! Are you up for a little cattle rustling?"

"Don't they hang people for cattle rustling?"

"Oh come on, Rox. We haven't lynched a rustler in Montana in a long time. Months. Come on. You have to take risks for true love."

The next day was Wednesday, a fact not lost on Christopher as he sat in literature class, staring blankly at the Shakespeare anthology on his desk.

It was Wednesday. And since it was afternoon, you had to say that Wednesday was already partly over, which meant it was practically Thursday. Thursday was the day before Friday.

75

Christopher ticked off the hours in his head. It was approximately fifty-two hours till he would pick Rox up at her house and drive her to the dance. Fifty-two hours before he would arrive—in his beat-up pickup—in front of the Maslow home, a building so large that it could probably house half the population of Longhorn, one to a room.

At least that's what Michael had told him at lunch. He'd said that Christopher's own house— the entire house—could probably fit comfortably in the formal dining room at the Pecos Pete Ranch. That image had really stuck in Christopher's mind. Other things Michael had told him had had an impact, too.

He glanced forward, toward the front of the class. She was there of course, wearing one of the wispy little dresses she favored. Her legs were stuck slightly out in the aisle, casually crossed, ankle over ankle, with one foot twisted sideways.

He really wished she would wear pants. Having to look at her legs absolutely destroyed his concentration. No one should have legs so perfect, so white, so beautifully formed, so obviously smooth as . . . as something. Michael would know what they were as smooth as.

On Friday, when he picked Rox up at her house, he might well have to exchange pleasantries with her father. According to Michael, he was a genius. A very rich, very powerful, completely ruthless genius who was known to reduce major movie stars to pools of quivering jelly.

Back when he'd been going with Julia Ardmore, he'd had to exchange pleasantries with Mr. Ardmore. But Mr. Ardmore owned the hardware store and Christopher knew him well. You could say Mr. Ardmore was a genius at finding just the right nut or bolt in his shop, but that was a little different.

It just wasn't worth it, Christopher realized. It was true. It had hit him with the suddenness of a revelation—it wasn't worth it. All the nerves and worry, all for a date. It was nuts. He'd had to rely on Michael to get him through a simple phone call. What was he going to do on Friday night? Rox would talk a blue streak, witty and clever and fascinating and intelligent and charming, and he would stand there with an expression of confusion and terror and utter stupidity like a calf caught in fence wire.

The bell rang, loud and sudden, and Christopher lurched violently. His books went skittering off his desk onto the floor.

Everyone was heading for the door in the usual last-period rush to freedom. Christopher bent over to get his things. Two white, perfect, smooth-as-something-or-other legs stopped just before him. He absolutely did not dare to look up.

"Hey, Christopher," Rox said.

"Hi," he muttered, keeping his eyes fixed on the floor as he collected his books very, very slowly.

"Listen, it seems some of your cattle have strayed over onto our range. Darby says it's about eight or nine head. They're bunched up in a little box canyon."

77

Christopher had collected all his books. He stood, but kept his eyes averted from her face. "That happens sometimes," he said. "Strays."

"Oh, I know." She laughed gaily and rested her hand lightly on his upper arm for just a fleeting moment. "I'm not such a dude I don't know *that*. I was just thinking what I'd do is drive them back over."

Christopher hesitated. She had said *drive*. Now, anyone around here would know that meant driving, as with a horse and a rider, urging the steers along. But for a fleeting moment he wondered if Rox meant *drive,* as in a car. No, she'd been here for a year. Surely . . .

"You say you would drive them across?" he said, looking at her at last with a skeptical squint.

"I've been learning to be a regular cowgirl," Rox said, a little defensively. "Darby's been teaching me. Although I'd like to learn more."

"Well, maybe what I'll do is I could just head on over this afternoon. Round 'em up myself, if you don't mind that."

"Great," she said happily. "I'll meet you there along the fence, by the pond."

"Meet me there?" he said. He could feel the blood draining out of his face.

"Me and Drifter. Then *you* can show me how it's done. I'm sure you're better at it than Darby is."

And then she was gone, leaving behind a scent like heaven and a laugh like the sound angels must make.

Christopher realized that he was alone in the

classroom. Alone except for Julia Ardmore, who was just leaving.

He looked past her into the hallway and spotted Michael walking past, instantly recognizable by the fact that he still walked at a speed appropriate for Manhattan at rush hour.

Christopher sprang into action. He brushed past Julia with a quick "Excuse me, Julia" and grabbed Michael roughly by the arm. He pinned the startled Michael against the lockers and began pleading.

Julia couldn't hear the gist of the frantic conversation between Christopher and Michael, but the fact that they were talking at all, let alone urgently—let alone urgently just seconds after Christopher had been panicked by something Rox Maslow said—definitely held her attention.

"Christopher MacAvoy and Michael Serrano," Julia muttered to herself. "Christopher MacAvoy and Rox Maslow."

She shook her head, trying to make sense of it, watching with her shrewd, almost clear eyes as Christopher and Michael walked away, still in deep conversation.

"Definitely out of the ordinary. Definitely not normal," she said. She raised one sculpted eyebrow. A ghost of a smile tugged at a corner of her mouth. "Opportunity?" she asked, trying out the word. She nodded slightly and answered her own question. "Yes, could be opportunity."

Chapter Eight

A STEADY BREEZE ruffled the green-and-golden grass. The mountains loomed gray and shadowed, with the sun still high but well past peak. Christopher sat on his horse's back, wearing a clean shirt, newly pressed jeans, and boots strangely free of their usual coating of mud. He was sitting stiffly in the saddle, and the horse sensed his uneasiness and became uneasy herself, casting her head around, snorting and sniffing the wind, looking for the threat that had made her rider so tense.

Then, with her sharp hearing, she noticed a tiny strange noise and cocked her ears back toward Christopher, trying to make sense of what sounded like . . . and yet unlike . . . a human voice.

The breeze caught Christopher's blond hair and blew it back from his ear. He quickly resettled his hat in such a way as to keep that from happening again. Because in his right ear was a tiny pink earphone, completely invisible under his hair. From it a wire looped over the top of his ear down the back of his neck, taped there by a one-inch piece of duct tape that was going to hurt a little when he took it off. The wire went on down, over his collarbone and crossing his right pectoral, where it was held in place by a piece of tape that was really, really going to hurt when he took it off. The wire joined a small black box, no bigger than a pack of cigarettes, that was stuck inside the waist of his jeans.

"Okay, sound check," the tiny voice said in his ear. *"Can you hear me okay?"*

"Yes, I can hear you. Can you hear me?" Christopher asked, speaking, as far as his horse could tell, to her.

"Perfect," Michael's voice said. *"No problem. Just like I told you. As long as you don't get out of range."*

"Okay," Christopher said tersely. "Isn't everyone with a CB or a shortwave going to hear everything?"

"Not at this low power," Michael said reassuringly. *"We only have a range of about a mile. Someone would have to be on just the right frequency and be within a mile of us. Relax. We're in the middle of a billion miles of cows and sheep and bears. Who in hell is going to be monitoring us?"*

"Guess you're right," Christopher said. "Oh . . . oh . . . here she comes."

"Get a grip, cowboy, it's all going to be fine," Michael's voice said in his ear.

At least she was wearing jeans, not a dress. He was relieved about that. There was some hope that he might be able to concentrate.

She waved. He waved back. She sent her horse into a canter. She rode well, he noticed. Not at all like the sack of potatoes most of the California people looked like on a horse. No, she rode well, moving like a part of the horse, graceful, a song.

He exhaled loud and long.

She smiled as she came near, slowed her horse, and reined him to a stop a few feet away. "Hi," she said.

"Hi," he said.

"Beautiful day, isn't it?" she said.

Any day with you is a beautiful day, Christopher thought to himself. But of course he just gulped, until a voice in his ear said, *"It's an especially beautiful day now."*

And Christopher said, "It's especially a beautiful day now."

Rox blushed a little at the compliment and seemed, to Christopher's eyes at least, to be pleasantly surprised.

"That's a very sweet thing to say," Rox said. She smiled at him, and he realized it didn't make all that much difference if her legs were bare or covered. It wasn't just a question of her legs. It was her. Every part of her. Some force emanated from her, some force that drew him to her and at the same time filled him with a sense of hopelessness.

"Guess we best get after those strays," he said.

The voice in his ear said, *"You sure you want to play cowboy right now? Try and kiss her."*

"No!" Christopher blurted.

"No?" Rox asked.

"I mean, yes," Christopher said. "To you, yes." He forced a shaky smile. "To anyone else it would be no."

"That made no sense."

And judging from Rox's puzzled expression, she clearly seemed to agree.

Christopher took a deep breath and urged his horse into an easy trot. Rox followed him.

"That's a beautiful horse," Rox said. "She's a mare, right?"

Christopher nodded. "I got her last year after Pete got too old and his legs started stiffening up on cold days. I've had Pete since I was a kid."

There, he told himself guardedly, this isn't so bad. They were having a conversation.

"Pete, huh? This is Drifter." Rox leaned forward and patted her horse on the neck.

Christopher nodded companionably. "This here is—" He stopped dead.

His horse's name was Roxana.

"What?" Rox pressed. "What's her name?"

"It really is a fine day," Christopher said, hoping his brilliant blush wasn't too obvious.

"I think we've covered this ground. It's a swell day."

"Yes, it's lovely," Rox said. "So what did you say your horse's name was?"

"She's um . . . She's . . ."

"Jeez, Christopher, I can't help you here. I don't know the horse's name. Don't you know your horse's . . . Ah! It's Roxana, isn't it? Good grief."

"She's Millie," Christopher said suddenly. "I named her after my mom," he lied.

"That's nice," Rox said. "I'd like to meet your mom someday. I guess you'll be meeting my dad this Friday."

"Uh-huh," Christopher said guardedly.

"I'm really looking forward to it."

"I'm really looking forward to it," Christopher parroted.

"He's a great man."

"He's a great man."

"And I really loved his work on Let Freedom Scream," Michael said.

"And I really loved his work on *Let Freedom Ring.*" This wasn't going to be so difficult. Why, it was—

Rox tilted her head to look at him. "Did you say *Let Freedom Ring?*"

"I believe I did."

"Christopher, don't you ever go to the movies?"

"What?" Christopher asked, now thoroughly confused.

"Because it wasn't *Let Freedom Ring,*" Rox said.

"I loved it," Christopher said desperately. The

85

day seemed suddenly much warmer. He was a fool! It was all going to come apart right now. He couldn't—

"It's Let Freedom Scream. *Scream!"* Michael yelled.

"You're saying *Let Freedom Ring,* right?" Rox asked again.

Don't panic. That was the important thing—don't panic. "Absolutely," Christopher reiterated. "My favorite movie—*Let Freedom Ring.*"

"No, you idiot. Scream. Scream!"

"Aaaaahhhhh!" Christopher screamed.

"No!"

"What's the matter?" Rox cried. Her horse had started at his scream and was eyeing Christopher nervously.

"It's Let Freedom Scream. *Listen to me."*

"I was . . . screaming," Christopher said lamely.

"Why?"

"Why? Why did I scream?"

"Because you were so . . . because, um . . . okay, you screamed because you suddenly were aware of just how fantastic it was to be with her. You screamed because of her."

"You made me scream. I mean . . . I mean . . . Um, could we just start over?" Christopher said, practically weeping with frustration. "What I meant was, being here with you . . . It's like something that I wanted. For a long time."

"That's not what I said."

"And now you're disappointed?" Rox said. Hurt

lurked just below the surface of her expression.

"Disappointed? No. Never. I was dot dot dot overwhelmed. And I swear if you say 'dot dot dot' I'll scream myself."

"Disappointed?" Christopher said. "No. Never. Never, not with you. I was . . . overwhelmed."

"Good boy."

Christopher drew what felt like his first breath in ten minutes.

Julia Ardmore was a cheerleader, and some people made the mistake of believing this meant she was perhaps less intelligent than some other girls. They were wrong.

Not that Julia worried much about what others thought of her. If they wanted to believe she was a cheering bimbo, fine. She had a 3.95 grade point average, and had scored 1,300 points on her preliminary SATs.

Julia kept her grades up with almost no studying. She didn't usually need to study, because she had been born with an excellent, near-photographic memory and a finely developed curiosity. She liked learning. And she liked learning things she wasn't supposed to learn.

It was a sort of game, watching all the little things that went on at school, in town, in church, and putting all the tiny observations together, things that seemed insignificant at first but, when all the dots were connected, painted a picture.

Dot number one—Rox Maslow arrives at

school in Christopher MacAvoy's truck. Dot number two—Christopher has lunch with Michael Serrano. Dot number three—in lit class Christopher nearly swallows his tongue when Rox mentions that some Three Aces strays are over on her father's land. Which was immediately followed by dot number four—Christopher grabs Michael and they have a very intense conversation.

Dot number five—Julia had followed Michael from town, which led to dot number six, which . . .Well, dot number six was right before her eyes.

Julia was in her father's dusty green pickup truck. She was high atop a ridge at the far edge of the Pecos Pete Ranch, just below the crest so she wouldn't be silhouetted, down in the shadows where she could see without being seen.

And what she saw was extraordinary.

A half mile to the west were two people on horses, Rox Maslow and Christopher MacAvoy. And about a quarter of a mile to the east from where she sat was an open-topped Jeep, parked in the middle of empty pastureland.

Every few minutes the Jeep would start up, move forward a hundred or two hundred feet, and stop again.

Michael Serrano was the person in the Jeep. The sight of Michael in a Jeep, out in the middle of nowhere, seeming to creep along at a safe distance just out of sight of Rox and Christopher, was simply too interesting and strange to be anything but trouble.

"Yes," Julia said to herself, "but what kind of trouble? What does it mean?" She rummaged in the cluttered glove compartment and was gratified to find the binoculars. She aimed and focused. The profile of Michael Serrano leapt into clear view.

He was holding something. A microphone. CB or shortwave.

"What on earth?"

Julia flipped on the two-way radio. The truck was used for making deliveries all over the valley, and her father liked to be able to stay in touch. Julia slowly began turning the radio's dials. Static. Static. Someone far off speaking in French. Static. Static. Then . . .

". . . *like you were born in a saddle,*" one male voice said.

"*You know, you ride like you were born in a saddle,*" a different male voice said.

Then, much more faint, but audible still, a female voice: "*That means a lot coming from you, Christopher. I'm looking forward to getting some pointers on driving these strays. I hope you don't mind answering a bunch of dumb questions.*"

The first male voice: "*You aren't capable of asking a dumb question.*"

Second male voice: "*You aren't even able to ask a dumb question.*"

The female voice laughed. Then: "*Oh, you just wait and see. You'll get tired of me.*"

The first male voice: "*Rox, I'd have to be tired of life to be tired of you.*"

89

The second male voice: *"Rox, I reckon I'd, um . . . I reckon I'd have to be tired of living before I'd be tired of you."*

The first male voice, wearily: *"Would you stop adding 'I reckons' to everything?"*

Julia sat with her mouth hanging open. She listened awhile longer. Rox and Christopher advanced further and the signal weakened a bit. Then Michael started the Jeep and moved forward. Julia's reception broke up into disjointed bits of conversation.

But she didn't really need to hear any more.

She started chuckling. "Oh, Christopher, Christopher, Christopher," she said, shaking her head. "You poor thing."

Then she started laughing some more, even wiping away a tear. "Serrano, you are such a bastard."

She started the truck and made a wide turn back toward town, smiling to herself and knowing she could use this to her own advantage.

Chapter Nine

WHEN ROX GOT home, Keanu Reeves was in the living room, sipping a cold drink and looking small in one of the huge easy chairs. Craig Maslow was pacing back and forth in front of the actor. He had a plastic bottle of springwater in one hand and was gesturing with the other.

"Hi, Keanu," Rox said. She gave a little wave and went upstairs to change. By the time she'd come back down the actor was gone.

"So, is he going to do the movie?" Rox asked her father.

Craig Maslow nodded. "I think so. It would be a big career move for him. He'd be following in the footsteps of José Ferrer and Gerard Depardieu." He gave his daughter a hug. "Where have you been, anyway?"

"Out rounding up strays and driving them back

over to the Three Aces," Rox said casually. She felt rather proud of the fact that she had participated in what amounted to an actual cattle drive. Kind of. The horses and Christopher had done most of the actual work.

Her father cocked a skeptical eyebrow. "You know, we have plenty of help to take care of things like that."

"I enjoyed it," Rox said.

"You and Darby?" her father pressed.

"Not exactly." Rox grinned coyly.

"Oh, I get it. So who is this young man?"

"You don't know him. His name is Christopher MacAvoy. You know, from the Three Aces Ranch. The neighbors on the southeast side?" When her father continued to look blank, she said, "Anyway, I'm going out with him Friday, and he's going to pick me up here. If you're going to be here, could you try to be nice to him?"

"When have I not been nice?" Her father pretended to be wounded.

"I mean, you know, try and sound normal. Don't talk about raising zebras, for example. And don't use the *F* word, the *M* word, the *A* word or the *J* word, or any of that."

"What *J* word?" he wondered.

"And don't do anything like offer to buy him a car or get him a part in a movie. He's very sweet and normal. And please, please don't do that thing where you ask him if he knows to use condoms."

"That was *one* time," Mr. Maslow complained.

92

"And I had just done that AIDS movie. I mean, Je—." He stopped. "Oh, *that J* word."

"Duh."

He grinned and shook his finger at her. "Don't you 'duh' me, young lady. Listen." He put his arm around her shoulder and walked her toward the kitchen. "The film festival is only ten days away, and I've been thinking that some of the locals don't seem all that enthusiastic about the event."

Rox said nothing, just rolled her eyes.

"What?" her father asked.

"You said I shouldn't 'duh' you anymore," Rox said. "Most of the locals really hate the film festival."

"Why?" They had reached the kitchen. Rox opened the refrigerator doors and the two of them contemplated the offerings. "I mean, the festival brings a lot of money into town, fills all the motels and hotels and restaurants. Besides, you mean to tell me these people don't like getting to see Jack Nicholson and Robert Redford walking around town?"

"Daddy, they probably could get used to it, only you set it up for the same weekend as the Longhorn Rodeo. All the hotels and motels and restaurants are full of Hollywood phonies, and I hate to tell you, but the people around here are much more excited about seeing some championship bull rider walking around than they are about Robert Redford. How about that pasta salad?"

"Yep." He grabbed the bowl. "Yeah, I realize the festival conflicts with the rodeo and I'm sorry about that. Maybe next year they can move the date of the rodeo."

Rox sighed. "Daddy, this is exactly why the locals don't like us. The rodeo has been on that date for about ninety years. This is only the second film festival."

Mr. Maslow dished out the pasta salad. "So I'm right. The locals don't like the festival."

"You know how you don't like it when *Entertainment Weekly* does its list of the most influential people in Hollywood and you're only like number three or something? That's how much the locals don't like the festival."

"I don't care what that trivial, hack-written rag has to say," Mr. Maslow sneered. "No one who's anyone really believes Spielberg is bigger than me. Not since the eighties." He thought a moment and munched a mouthful of broccoli, yellow peppers, and tubetti. "But I get your point. They don't like being made to feel like a sideshow in their own town. That's why I'm thinking of some way to get more local involvement. I want to get some of the local folks to act as presenters, you know, along with the usual celebrity types. See, then, if Cousin Ed from the feed store and Aunt Petunia from the altar guild are going to be in the show, running lines with Sharon and Robin, giving out awards to Jack or Bobby or Meryl, or even to me, well, then they're involved, right? And we'll even pay them."

Rox considered the idea for a minute. Setting aside the snide reference to Aunt Petunia, it might not be the worst idea her father had ever had. "Maybe," she said. "Maybe it wouldn't be a bad idea."

"Great. It's a deal. In fact, you know what? We'll sign up your friend Christopher, first thing."

"So?" Darby demanded. "Kiss?"

"No kiss," Rox said. "Can we concentrate on our homework?" Rox and Darby were in Rox's room. Open schoolbooks, open notebooks, a thesaurus, a dictionary, a bag of Doritos, and Rox herself were strewn across the bed. Darby had pulled a chair up next to the bed and had her feet propped on the headboard.

"Are you kidding? Study? Yeah, right. Not till I get all the good stuff."

"Look, there was no kiss, all right?" Rox said, feeling annoyed.

"Did he try?"

"No."

Darby thought for a moment. She shook her head like a doctor who doesn't like the look of the mole she's examining. "So . . . what *did* you guys do?"

"We rounded up the strays and drove them back over to his ranch. That *was* the plan, after all."

Darby made a derisive snorting sound. "Uh-huh. That was the plan. That's why you and I went and stole those cows in the first place, so you could just calmly drive them back the next day."

"I thought they were steers, not cows," Rox said.

"I thought the plan was to get to know him better before the big date."

"I do know him better," Rox said.

"Just not *better.* You think he doesn't like you?"

Rox shrugged. "He sounds like he likes me. I mean, the things he says, it's like . . . I don't know, like we're one of those couples on *The Young and the Restless.* He says all these amazing things. He kind of, you know, says a lot, really."

"Wait a minute. This is Christopher MacAvoy we're talking about, right? Let me remind you—my *father* says Christopher is a young man of few words, and my father's entire vocabulary is 'yup' and 'nope.' My mom says he proposed to her by saying, 'We best get hitched.'"

Rox slammed her book shut suddenly. "I know, I know. It is weird." She got up from the bed and began pacing. "For a year he won't even say hello, right? Then the first time I talk to him all he can do is grunt and stutter. Okay, he was seminaked at the time, so I understand."

"If he'd been raised right, he'd have tipped his hat to a lady," Darby said, grinning.

"Then I drive to school with him—"

"—after tricking him into picking you up."

"—and again, he has very little to say. But that's fine, because he is who he is, and that's the guy I like so much. I'm thinking it would help if maybe he could at least learn to say 'hi' and 'how are you' and 'do you want to go out,' but I'm willing to be patient."

"Patient, right. That would explain why you tricked him into picking you up."

"Well, someone had to get things started," Rox said. "But now! It's like I got him started and he won't stop. At least, he won't stop talking. Everything I say, he's got this big, flowery speech ready. It's sweet, really. But . . ." She flopped her hands to her side in frustration.

"Maybe he's kept it all locked up inside all these years, and now he's letting it out. Some guys are like that. They're like all bottled up because they think they can't ever show their true emotions or whatever. If you'd watch Ricki Lake, you'd know these things."

"I liked him more when he was all bottled up," Rox said. "I mean, I still like him, but it's like now I like him in spite of himself, you know?"

"No, I don't."

"Today, riding out to that box canyon with him, you know what I really wanted?" Rox said wistfully. "I wanted to listen to the birds and the wind and the sound the horses' hooves make."

"And then lip lock," Darby said.

Rox ignored her. "And, okay, I would have liked to talk to him, just like a normal person. You know, just about normal stuff. What does he want to be when he graduates? Is he going to college? Usual stuff."

"And then lip lock," Darby said.

"And after we talked awhile, and enjoyed the scenery, and he showed me how to rope cows—"

"Then lip lock?"

"Exactly."

"So tell him how you feel about him. Say, 'Look, Christopher, I really like you a lot, but I'd appreciate it if you'd just shut up and kiss me.'"

Rox laughed. "That's about what I *would* like to say. Only now I can't say it because you've already said it."

"Go ahead, who's going to know?"

"Right. Like I would try and get a guy to kiss me by using someone else's words." Rox sat back down. "So guess what? My dad has this brilliant new idea to get some local people to help out at the film festival. He wants me to ask Christopher to do it."

Darby made a snorting sound. "No way. It's the same night as the rodeo."

"Yeah, I know. I'm not even going to mention it. It would just be mean making him choose between going with me to something he'd hate and going to the rodeo."

"Besides, he'd choose rodeo over you. I don't care *how* romantic he's suddenly gotten."

"Actually, I wish I could go to the rodeo with him. But Daddy expects me to be at the festival, and I kind of have to." She lay back on the bed and stared up at the ceiling. "Just the same, it would be nice, being with Christopher at the rodeo. I want to do all the things he likes to do, and be with him in places where he's happy. I have the feeling that's where he's happiest. He was talking about it today. He tried twice to ride bulls and both times he didn't make it. He's determined to do it, though. It would be great to be there when he does. I mean, *that's* the real Christopher, I think—a guy who works really hard and is good and honest and decent and, for some reason, likes trying to ride bulls that don't want to be ridden."

"You sound like you're talking about some different person from the one you were with today."

Rox shrugged. "Mostly, like when we were just riding, or when he was showing me how to swing a rope, or sometimes when he would just say some little thing, he was the Christopher I thought he was. Other times . . . I don't know. Other times, it's like he reminds me of someone else. Only I can't figure out who."

"Well, I don't guess *either* Christopher would want to go to your dad's film festival."

"No." Rox laughed and opened her book again. "I wouldn't even ask him, unless I deliberately wanted to make him miserable."

Chapter Ten

O N THURSDAY, IN addition to his chores and his homework, Christopher cleaned his truck from front bumper to back. He polished his pair of good black boots till they shone. He brushed and shaped his best hat, holding the brim over a jet of steam coming from a kettle on the kitchen stove. He spent a good while trying to get his fingernails entirely clean and all trimmed to the same length.

On Friday morning he did all his chores before school, careful to wear gloves at all times and keep his fingernails in their new, pristine state. He threw a tarp over the bed of the truck to keep it clean and put off a job involving fertilizer until the date was safely over.

After school on Friday he drove straight home and changed into his cleanest jeans, his polished boots, and his pressed and starched shirt. He combed his hair and shaved the few whiskers that grew on his chin. He applied Mennen aftershave, and looked at himself in the bathroom mirror.

He had never seen a more depressing sight. His hair was too long, but he couldn't cut it, not with the need to conceal the earpiece. But more worrisome than his hair was the sick expression on his face. He looked like a man preparing to make the long final walk to the electric chair.

"You're scared," he admitted to his reflection. It was dumb to worry, because after all, he had Michael in his ear the whole time, whispering the right words to make Rox happy—at least early on. But Michael couldn't help him with dancing. Christopher knew exactly one dance—the two-step. And he wasn't even good at that.

And then there was the kiss.

The very thought made him sick from the combination of violent emotions—fear and desire and more fear and still more desire. At one moment he would gladly trade the ranch and his right arm for the chance to press his lips gently against hers. And that feeling was as powerful and irresistible as the movement of the earth on its axis. But the next instant that same thought, that same imagined kiss, made him want to break out in hysterical giggles and crawl under his bed.

Michael could not help him with the kiss.

But if you get to that part, he told himself grimly, *you have to tell her about Michael.* He would use Michael during the early stages of the date, but he couldn't use him to get a kiss. No. He couldn't kiss her under false pretenses. So if it looked like a kiss was even a possibility . . .

Yep. Tell her. And then she would slap him and stomp off and he wouldn't have to worry about kissing her.

He checked his watch. It was time.

He went out into the living room. His mother was watching *Hard Copy* and doing a jigsaw puzzle. She looked up at him and smiled.

"You look very nice, Christopher," she said.

"Thank you, ma'am," he said, attempting a casual, devil-may-care tone that just sounded desperate.

His mother laughed. "It's a date, honey. Try and look like you're going to a dance, not a funeral. Smile."

"Yes, ma'am," he said. He forced a smile.

His mother winced. "Maybe you don't have to smile."

He nodded.

"So this is some special girl, huh?"

He was startled. "Special?" How did she know that Rox was special?

His mother got up and came over to straighten his collar. "I can tell," she said. "With you MacAvoy men, the amount you care is in direct proportion to how terrified and nauseous you look."

Christopher laughed, a genuine laugh that diminished his tension a little. "I reckon she must be special, then," he said.

"Well, she's a lucky girl," his mother said. "Any girl's lucky to be going out with you. Who is she?"

"Rox Maslow."

"Craig Maslow's daughter?" his mother asked, eyes suddenly wide.

"Yes, ma'am."

"Well . . . don't you worry, she's still a lucky girl," his mother said, trying hard to conceal her own doubts.

Christopher sighed deeply.

To Christopher's relief, the meeting with Craig Maslow was brief and uneventful. Mr. Maslow said hello. Christopher said hello back. They shook hands. He seemed, to Christopher's surprise, like a normal sort of person. He asked what time Christopher expected to have Rox home, and Christopher told him. He gave Christopher a bit of a fish eye and told him he didn't want to hear that Christopher had been drinking and then driving.

"I don't drink, sir," Christopher said.

"Not at all?" Mr. Maslow asked, nonplussed.

"No, sir."

"Huh," Mr. Maslow said thoughtfully. "You know, you can cut the 'sirs.' Call me Craig."

"I don't reckon I could do that, sir," Christopher said.

"You like movies?"

Christopher shrugged. "I don't see a whole lot. I'll watch an old Clint Eastwood picture on TV sometimes. Or else the Duke."

Maslow laughed, but not unkindly. "Why am I not surprised that you'd be a Clint Eastwood and

John Wayne fan? How about Dayton Hill?"

Christopher looked up sharply. "I reckon that's the one movie star I would truly love to meet," he said.

"He's the Clint Eastwood for the nineties," Mr. Maslow said. "He's going to bring back the cowboy picture all by himself. Did you know his last movie grossed a hundred and ten million? And we're just talking domestic revenues. He's *huge* in the Middle East and South America, with that whole macho thing they have going. Huge."

"Yes, sir," Christopher said, having no clear idea what Mr. Maslow was talking about. "I do admire Mr. Dayton Hill."

Just then, Rox came down the stairs and stopped the conversation dead.

She was wearing a short dress that revealed several miles of leg and was made of some kind of silky substance that seemed more liquid than any fabric should be.

He was torn between a desire to either bow down and worship her, throw his hat in the air and yell "Yahoo!," or run for the door and disappear into the night.

It was impossible, he thought, that such beauty could exist in a world filled with ordinary mortals such as he. Some basic law of the universe was being violated here. It was ludicrous to imagine that she was even part of the human race as he knew it. Still more insane to expect that she would choose to spend her time with him.

"Hi, Christopher," she said happily. She went to

her father and gave him a kiss on his cheek. "You haven't been cross-examining Christopher, have you?"

"So far I've discovered he's polite, respectful, expects to have you home two hours earlier than I was going to demand, and doesn't drink," Mr. Maslow said. "Every father's nightmare," he joked.

"He didn't mention that little murder conviction, though, did he?" Rox teased.

"Plus," Mr. Maslow added, "he's a big Dayton Hill fan, which is a lot more reassuring than if he'd been a Charlie Sheen fan."

Christopher led the way out to his truck. It was parked between one of the Land Rovers and a red Lamborghini.

He held the passenger side door open for Rox and took her hand to help her climb up into the seat.

Christopher went around and climbed in beside her. Thankfully, the engine started without too much grinding and coaxing.

This is so wrong, Christopher realized. *I belong with her about as much as I belong sipping tea with the queen of England.* If only Michael were here. But Christopher had decided he could handle the drive into town all on his own. What a fool he had been! Now he had nothing to say. He was sitting beside a girl who was from another universe, a different species, a creature made of everything that was fine and flawless and brilliant. He couldn't love her. He could only worship from afar.

"I haven't been to one of these dances before," Rox said. "What are they like?"

"Um . . . well, they're pretty much just regular dances. Nothing special."

"Do you think this dress is okay?" Rox asked. "I wasn't sure how formal or informal to be."

"The dress?" he said, not wanting to think too much about the dress.

She looked concerned. "Oh, no. It's wrong, isn't it? Too much? Too showy? Is that it?"

He clutched the wheel. If only Michael's voice were in his ear right now. Michael would know what to say.

"We can turn around," Rox said suddenly. "Go back and I'll change into something else."

"No," he said.

"I don't want to embarrass you," Rox said.

"You . . . you don't embarrass me," he said finally.

Rox looked a little hurt. "Well, that's quite an endorsement," she said, pouting just a little. "I don't *embarrass* you."

"You . . ." He took a deep breath. "You don't embarrass me. You . . . you . . . you scare me a little."

"Scare you?" She thought this over for a moment. "Why would I scare you?"

His eyes flickered toward her. "Because . . . I don't know the words."

She smiled. "You always seem to know the words, once you get started."

Once Michael Serrano tells me what to say, Christopher thought grimly. *Only he isn't here.*

"The thing is . . . you remember that story we had last year? The one about what's-his-name . . . Icarus?"

107

"Sure," Rox said. "He wanted to fly, so he made himself some wings. But then he flew too near to the sun and was destroyed."

Christopher nodded. "That's the story. Ordinary guy tries to fly and ends up falling back down to earth."

Rox laughed. "But what does that have to do with us? Icarus flew too near the sun. It's nighttime."

Christopher nodded. "The thing is . . . you *are* the sun."

Rox smiled, a little sadly. "That is an extremely sweet thing to say. Now would you do me a favor and pull over?"

"Pull over? Oh. You want me to take you home."

"No, I want you to pull over onto the side of the road."

Christopher did as she asked.

"Now turn off the lights and the engine," Rox instructed.

Christopher did that, too. The silence of the night fell around them. Overhead the sky was an explosion of stars. A cool breeze blew down the valley, clean and smelling of grass and black soil.

"This is our first real date, I guess," Rox said. "But we went riding the other day, right? So in some ways this could be our second date."

Christopher said nothing. He waited, expecting the kind- but-dismissive words that would consign him to oblivion, far away from her.

"And I know around here girls aren't supposed to be aggressive or anything, but I don't think this date is going to work out very well unless we clear something up first."

Christopher nodded solemnly. *Clear something up first—you've made a terrible mistake and you want me to drive you home. I understand.*

"The thing is, Christopher, I want you to kiss me."

Christopher nodded again. *Kiss you. Yes, I understand. You want—*

"What?"

"You heard me," Rox said. "I would like you to kiss me."

Christopher heard a whimpering sound come from his throat.

"Are you going to kiss me or not?" Rox demanded. "A simple yes or no. You don't have to be all poetic about it. Yes or no?"

Christopher took a deep breath that delivered exactly zero oxygen to his brain. He recognized the emotion he was feeling, and it did not make him proud. It was fear. Absolute terror. Like the first time he had climbed on a bull's back. He'd been thrown off in less than two full seconds. It had been painful and humiliating. He'd been afraid then, too, and it had turned out just as badly as he'd feared.

She was just two feet away, leaning back against the seat, her head turned to face him. Her eyes watched him solemnly. She swallowed, almost as if she were nervous, too. She bit her lip as if she were uncertain. She was waiting for him to say yes or no.

"Yes," he said, and felt his insides lurch.

She turned toward him. He noticed the way her

dress clung to her body. He noticed the way one of her knees now pressed against his thigh. He noticed that quite a bit.

He was falling, falling toward her, down a deep, dark well. Falling into her gravity, no longer able to resist. He could feel her breath on his face. He could feel the warmth from her skin. He could see nothing but her eyes, and could still see them even after he closed his own.

His lips touched hers. The breeze stopped blowing, the world stopped turning, every living thing held its breath.

Her lips were hot and soft and trembling. She opened them, just a little.

He was burning up. He was screaming inside his head. His heart was hammering. Every muscle in his body tensed and shivered. He had the definite sense that he might, at any moment, simply explode.

She pulled back.

He breathed, for what felt like the first time in an hour.

"That was nice," she said, in a voice several octaves lower than usual. "And now that we have *that* settled, we can get on with going to the dance. Now we can just be normal."

But of course Christopher knew she was wrong. He would never be normal again. He was lost. He was destroyed. He was Icarus plunging toward the earth.

He was in love.

Chapter Eleven

CHRISTOPHER HAD ENTIRELY forgotten the earphone concealed in his hair by the time they reached town. In fact, he had forgotten his own name several times. But he was reminded of both pieces of information when Michael Serrano's New York-inflected voice suddenly erupted in his ear.

"Christopher, buddy. I see your truck approaching. You okay, man?"

"Aah!" Christopher said suddenly. "Sorry," he said to Rox. "I bit my lip."

"I guess you're still alive. If you're okay, tap the mike twice. If you're panicked and you've already screwed everything up totally, tap it three times."

Christopher sneaked a sideways glance at Rox. She was looking out the window. He dropped his hand to his waist and tapped the transmitter twice.

111

"Gotcha. Cool. Have you told her how beautiful she is?"

Christopher considered for a moment. *Had* he told Rox she was beautiful? He'd certainly been thinking it. But had he told her? Probably not. And he *should* have, he chided himself bitterly. She was all dressed up, made up, with her hair done and all. He *should* have told her she was beautiful.

"Say . . . um . . . okay, say—Rox, you are beautiful beyond anything my imagination could have conjured up."

Christopher fidgeted a little in his seat. Somehow this didn't seem right anymore. Actually, it had never felt right, but it felt even less right now. Still, Michael knew what he was talking about, didn't he? Christopher should have told Rox how lovely she was.

"Um, Rox? I . . . I wanted to say that you are beautiful beyond anything my imagination could have conjured up."

To his surprise, Rox actually seemed a little troubled. A shadow passed across her face. "Thank you, Christopher. And by the way, you're looking good yourself."

They had reached the school. Kids were spilling from cars and trucks, guys dressed much like Christopher, girls in a wide variety of dresses, wearing high heels and carrying tiny purses.

Christopher parked and went around to open Rox's door. All over again she took his breath away.

As if reading Christopher's mind, Michael said, *"Tell her she takes your breath away."*

112

"You take my breath away," Christopher said as he took her hand to help her step down from the truck.

"You're not getting back into that thing where you're scared of me again, are you?" Rox asked playfully.

Christopher heard derisive laughter in his ear. *"You told her you were scared of her? Please, tell me you didn't say that. Now she'll totally own you!"*

"I guess I'll always be a little scared," Christopher said, for lack of any better answer, and since Michael was still laughing.

Rox put her arm around his waist and leaned in to give him just the lightest kiss on his lips. "There. I guess I'll have to do that every time you start looking too scared."

"She kissed you!"

Christopher fought the urge to spin around and try to spot Michael. Clearly Michael could see them. It was a little unnerving. It was also unnerving the way he seemed to be so loudly upset.

"She kissed you! What was that about? How did that happen? That's not even planned till much later. I thought we went over all this. Why did we have a plan if you're just going to blow it off?"

Michael shook his head. Great. He'd kissed her, all on his own. That was no good. Much more of that kind of thing and Christopher would start thinking he could get along on his own.

And it was vital that Christopher remain insecure. Vital.

Michael was in his car just fifty feet away, hidden by the darkness at the far end of the parking lot. His binoculars were trained on Christopher and Rox as they headed inside, melding with the crowd around the entrance to the gym. He could hear the faint beat of the music—some god-awful "country" noise. Cowboy music. Oh, the hicks would be stomping their boots and raising a ruckus in there soon, he thought contemptuously.

He could hear the music more clearly through the earphone. The music and the chattering of voices and, from time to time, Christopher's stomach growling hungrily.

He was rapidly losing the ability to hear Rox distinctly, and that worried him a little bit. Her voice was being drowned out by all the other noise. It required terrific concentration to follow what she was saying and come up with all the right responses for Christopher.

He really should be getting paid for this, he thought. But then, he reassured himself, he would be paid soon enough. That thought cheered him considerably.

He keyed the microphone. "Tell her she makes all these other girls look like horses," he said maliciously. "No, no, forget that." It wasn't time yet to let his true feelings out. A little while longer. "Tell her you feel invisible standing beside her, since every eye in the place must be on her."

He keyed the microphone off. "Not bad," he commented to himself. "Not a bad line. I can use that in a screenplay someday." He listened while Christopher delivered the line. Good enough. He strained to hear Rox's reaction. She seemed flattered. Good.

He took a sip from his bottle of Evian water. He keyed the microphone again. "Tell her that every guy in the place is eating his heart out with jealousy. Then, if she buys that okay, ask her to dance."

"Oh, she'll buy it," a voice said.

Michael jumped so high in his seat that he hit his head on the roof of the car. He spun around, eyes blazing. "Who?" He had to squint to focus in the dark. "Julia?"

Julia Ardmore went around to the far side of the car, opened the door, and slid onto the seat beside him.

He looked at her with undisguised horror. She was going to ruin everything. How had he not heard her walking up beside the car? How could he have been so careless? And was there any way to buy her silence?

"It took me a while to figure this out," Julia said conversationally. "You're really quite a rotten person, aren't you, Serrano?"

"Um, why don't you just get out," Michael blurted. He made a shooing gesture with his free hand. In his ear Rox was saying something to Christopher and Christopher was saying nothing at all in response.

"Okay," Julia said cheerily. "I'll get out. Then I'll go and tell Roxana all about this."

Michael let a cocky smile show. "Go right ahead. All I'm trying to do is help poor Christopher out. I mean, the boy is so totally tongue-tied. He begged me to help him get Rox interested in him." He held out his hands in a parody of innocence. "I'm just trying to be a friend to the poor guy."

To Michael's surprise, Julia laughed. It was a nice long laugh that showed off her perfect white teeth.

"Yeah, that's you all over, Serrano. Just trying to be a friend. That's what had me puzzled. See, I happened to follow you the other day when you were riding around and feeding lines to Christopher. At first I thought, hmm, what's Serrano doing out here in the open? I thought he lived under a rock."

"People have the wrong idea about me," Michael said.

"Then I saw you talking into a microphone. That very microphone," she said, pointing. "So I tuned my radio, and what do you know? It was Michael the love doctor. Then the question was— why, why, why?"

"Because I was trying to help, like I said."

"I considered that . . . for about two seconds. Then I asked myself, what's Serrano's angle? It took a while, but I figured it out. By the way, don't neglect your duties." She pointed at the microphone. "I wouldn't want Christopher to blow it now."

"They're dancing, not talking," Michael said. "Okay, so tell me—what's my 'angle,' as you put it?"

"Oh, you're after Rox Maslow. Except of course you're really after Craig Maslow. You don't care one way or the other about Rox. You're after Mr. Moneybags."

"You don't even know me, Julia," he said. "What

116

makes you think you have me all figured out?"

For a moment Julia seemed taken aback. She lowered her bold gaze and bit her lip. "I know more about you than you think, Serrano. I know you want to be a screenwriter, and that you've already applied to UCLA because you want to go to film school, and a connection to Craig Maslow would make life very easy for you in Hollyweird."

Michael was instantly suspicious. How did she know about him? What had she been doing, spying on him? She would have had to pump all his friends for information, and since he didn't have many friends . . .

"Anyway," Julia said. "I know the plan. See, Rox is attracted to Christopher, and vice versa. Rox thinks Christopher is some kind of Montana paragon. She thinks he's honest and straightforward and sweet and open. Especially honest, unlike . . . well, unlike certain people in this car. So you help bring Christopher and her together. Then, at just the right time, when she's fallen for him, you come forward and say, 'Look, it was all a fake! Christopher's a lying snake who used me to win you. It was all *my* truest emotions, spoken by Christopher, that made you fall in love. It's me, Michael, that you fell in love with, without knowing it.'"

Michael fidgeted uneasily. She had it right, and there wasn't much point in denying it. "I suppose now you're going to lecture me about what a jerk I am, right?"

"No."

"No?"

"No," Julia said. "I think it's brilliant. And it works fine for me. See, I used to go with Christopher. And I want him back."

Michael just stared at her. It was strange. He'd seen her in the halls at school, and cheerleading at games, and around in town. Yet they'd barely spoken before. And he'd certainly never before noticed that she was really quite beautiful.

But of course, he thought, true beauty comes from inside, and he hadn't really gotten a glimpse of her inside till now.

"So. When are you going to pull the plug and shatter Rox and Christopher's happy little world?" Julia asked. "I want to watch."

Yes, she really was quite pretty. "Tonight," he said. "As the dance comes to an end, and she is all aglow with the experience and beginning to think that she really does love him. That's the moment when I rip their little romance into shreds."

Michael laughed out loud, and Julia joined in. It was a disturbing sound.

Julia stayed with Michael for a while. He rigged it so she could hear all that he was hearing, and she sat beside him in the dark, listening to the conversation between Christopher and Rox.

She even helped, contributing lines when Michael began to tire of the constant demands of inventing sweet, romantic things to say.

"She's gone to the ladies' room," Michael observed. "We need something for when she gets back."

"Do you think he can handle a little poetry?" she asked Michael.

He shrugged. "Well, he's your former boy-friend. What do you think?"

"Let's give it a try," Julia said. "If it works, she'll love it. What girl doesn't like love poetry?"

"Okay." He listened for a moment. "He says she's coming back." He keyed the microphone. "Christopher? Get ready." He turned to Julia. "Okay, but don't talk while the mike is on."

And Julia said:

> She walks in beauty, like the night
> Of cloudless climes and starry skies;
> And all that's best of dark and bright
> Meet in her aspect and her eyes.

Michael raised an eyebrow in surprise but keyed the microphone and repeated the lines to Christopher, pausing at the end of each line. Christopher then repeated them to Rox.

"Nice," Michael complimented Julia.

"Lord Byron," Julia explained.

"Huh. If I'd known I'd have to do this someday, I guess I'd have read more poetry."

Julia put her hand on his arm, a reassuring gesture. "You're doing fine. Look, I'd better go inside for a while. My poor date is probably wondering what happened to me."

"Date, huh?" Michael said.

119

"Yeah. You know, just till I can get Christopher back."

"Okay, well, don't forget to be around when I stick it to the little lovebirds."

"I wouldn't miss it for anything in the world."

Julia climbed out of the car, bent back down to flash him a big smile, and walked exactly ten feet away. There she stopped and pretended to have a problem with her panty hose. She propped one leg high on the back of someone's truck, raised her skirt as high as she dared, and carefully smoothed the nylon up her leg. She had no doubt whatsoever that Michael would be watching.

"Take *that,* Serrano," she muttered under her breath.

It had been an extremely odd night, from Rox's point of view, composed of wildly different moments, incredible highs followed by disappointing lows, none of which came together to paint a single picture.

First had come the moment when she'd walked down the stairs and seen Christopher waiting there for her. A definite high. *Cute* was too cute a word to apply to him. He was handsome and strong and, despite the fact that he was clearly nervous, he managed to stand toe-to-toe with her father without seeming small or immature. A major accomplishment, since Rox had seen millionaire movie stars quiver and grovel in her father's presence.

Then there had been the kiss. If she lived a hundred more years, she would never forget that kiss. It wasn't the first time she had kissed a boy, but it might as well have been, because from that moment on, all other kisses were forgotten.

But then! Suddenly Christopher had started in with the romantic, poetic blah-blah-blah. Okay, it *was* sweet. Okay, it *was* sensitive. But it was getting to be way too much. She'd gone to the girls' room to exchange gossip with Darby, and when she'd come back, Christopher was actually reciting poetry!

Byron? Suddenly Christopher MacAvoy was quoting Byron? Poetry? From a guy who had not managed for the entire previous year to say more than two words to her?

It was bizarre. Not that she didn't appreciate the sentiment. It was hard not to be a little flattered when someone said you walked in beauty like the night. Still . . .

On the other hand, she loved it when they danced. Especially when, like now, it was a slow dance, and his arms were around her, and she could feel his sinewy, muscled body against her.

Wonderful, she realized, but what kind of a relationship could you have with a guy when you kept wishing he would shut up?

The music faded and they separated reluctantly.

"Rox, you make me feel like none of my life before tonight has had any meaning," Christopher said.

Rox nodded. "Thanks."

"I, uh, have to make a run to the boys' room," he said.

"If you gotta go, you gotta go," she joked, trying to lighten the mood.

"Every guy in the room will try and steal you away while I'm gone," he said.

"I'll be over by the punch," Rox said. She was ashamed when she sighed in relief that he was gone. She drifted toward the punch.

"Well, well, well. Hello, Rox," Julia said, materializing from the knot of bodies clustered around the cookies and punch.

"Hi, Julia," Rox said coldly. The last thing she needed was any grief from Julia Ardmore.

"Having a good time?" Julia asked.

"Yes. Excuse me, I want a drink."

"Certainly. It's thirsty work, all that . . . walking."

Rox peered at her. Julia was grinning like a cat with a helpless mouse in sight. "What walking?"

"You know, walking in beauty, like the night."

Rox froze. "What have you been doing, Julia, eavesdropping?"

Julia stepped closer and pitched her voice down, a low, urgent whisper. "I want to talk to you. *Before* Christopher gets back."

"What if I don't want to talk to you?"

"Look, I don't like you, you don't like me, but believe me on this, Rox. You *do* want to talk to me."

Chapter Twelve

THERE WAS A short line going into the boys' room, so Christopher waited. And while he waited, he tried to figure out what had gone wrong with the evening. Everything had been perfect early on. But since they'd gotten to the dance, Rox had seemed increasingly distracted. Even annoyed.

It must be his dancing. He should have asked Michael for some pointers on some cooler dances. He glanced back over his shoulder and, through the moving sea of heads, spotted Rox by the refreshments. Someone was talking to her. Julia Ardmore, it looked like. Well, good. At least she was talking to another girl and not a guy.

"Hey, Christopher," someone said. He focused. Tom Wagner, a friend of his.

"Hey, Tom. How's it going?"

"Can't complain," Tom said. He looked

Christopher over. "Here with Rox Maslow?"

"That's right," Christopher said. He braced for one of two reactions, either some crack about going out with a Hollyweirdo or else some indecent leering remark. In either case he would, reluctantly, have to invite Tom to step outside, which would be unfortunate, since Tom was a good six foot two and a fullback on the football team.

Fortunately, Tom said, "Guess it's a good thing, you and Rox Maslow together. There's been too much of people splitting into this group or that group and looking to be disagreeable. Besides, she *is* a vision." He nodded appreciatively. "So. You decide about signing up for the rodeo?"

Christopher was relieved. The rodeo was safer ground. "Thinking on it," he said. "My mother doesn't like the idea much. Doesn't want me breaking my neck."

Tom punched him good-naturedly in the arm. "Don't be such a mama's boy. Besides, you're pretty good. You stayed on for, what was it? Two whole seconds the last time you tried bull riding?"

"You ride bulls? What are you, crazy?"

Christopher made an angry face. Suddenly he really wished he could just turn off the annoying New York voice. He'd forgotten that Michael could still hear everything that was going on.

That was it. He was putting an end to this. As soon as he got back to Rox.

"Hey, don't get riled," Tom said, laughing. "Maybe it was three seconds."

Christopher laughed. "If I *do* sign up for this rodeo, it'll be the whole eight seconds."

"Just as long as they Velcro your skinny butt to the back of that bull it will be," Tom teased.

It took a few more minutes to get into the boys' room, finish, and wash his hands. As he washed his hands, Christopher stared long and hard at the face in the mirror. *I'm going to tell her,* he said silently, so as not to be overheard by Michael and half the boys in the school.

He marched back to her, full of determination.

Somehow, just during the few minutes he was gone, she had managed to grow even more beautiful. She met him with open arms. Literally. She put her arms around him and drew him close. She looked up into his face with an expression that was . . . unreadable. At first she'd almost looked mad, despite the warm greeting. But that couldn't be, because she was smiling a huge smile.

And yet her eyes . . .

"I'm so glad you're back," Rox said. "I missed you. I've gotten so I can't go any time at all without hearing you say one of the many romantic things you keep saying. Like that little bit of poetry you quoted? I loved that so much. It's so flattering. It's so exactly what a girl wants to hear. I could live on your beautiful words alone. Do you know any more poetry? Do you?"

Christopher just stared. He was no great student of women's emotions, but it sure seemed to him that she was being different. This was definitely some kind of emotion or other, but he wasn't sure which one.

The one thing he *was* sure of was that this was no time to tell her about Michael.

"Ha-ha! Guess she likes the patter, huh? Poetry, huh? Hang on just a minute."

Christopher stared and sweated and waited with Rox in his arms, still looking up at him with a gaze that was either loving or furious. "Um, poetry?" he said in an uncertain squeak.

"Poetry, yes. I love it when you quote poetry."

"Okay . . ."

"Shall I compare thee to a summer's day?"

"Shall I compare thee to a summer's day?"

"Thou art more lovely and more temperate."

"Thou art more lovely and more temperate."

"Shakespeare?" Rox asked.

"Um . . ."

"Yes. Try to get off the poetry, all right?"

"Yes. Shakespeare."

"More. I want more," Rox said, pressing her lips to Christopher's ear and sending shivers all up and down his body.

"More poetry?" Christopher stalled, panicking.

"Don't you know any more?" Rox asked. She made a pouting face.

"Oh, I know plenty more," Christopher said.

"For God's sake, Christopher, don't push it!"

"Don't use the Lord's name in vain," Christopher muttered under his breath.

"What did you say?" Rox asked, puzzled.

126

"Just clearing my throat," he said. "I have that poetry ready now," he announced, having heard Michael beginning to recite. Strange, but for a moment there, Christopher could have sworn he'd heard a girl's voice in his ear with Michael's.

"Oh, recite it for me," Rox pressed.

"Okay, well . . ."

> She was a phantom of delight
> When first she gleamed upon my sight;
> A lovely apparition, sent
> To be a moment's ornament.

Christopher sighed with relief. That had been tough. If he could get through that—

"That's lovely," Rox said. "Who wrote it?"

"Wordsworth."

"Woolworth's," Christopher said. No, wait. That couldn't be—

"No, you moron! Wordsworth!"

Christopher swallowed hard. "I mean, Wadsword."

"Wordsworth. William W–O–R–D–S–W—"

"William Woodsword."

"You're gonna make me swear! Listen to me— Wordsworth!"

"Do you mean Wordsworth?" Rox asked helpfully.

"That's what I said!"

"Christopher, why are you yelling at me?" Rox said, looking hurt.

"I'm not yelling at you," Christopher cried. "It's just—"

"You did not say Wordsworth, you practically said Wal-Mart, you—"

"It was Walmart. William Walmart."

"That's it. That does it. I am now going to take the Lord's name in vain. Several times."

"Is anything the matter, Christopher?" Rox asked. "You look a little sick. Look how your forehead is all sweaty. Are you sure you're all right?"

"Great, now you're having a heart attack. Tell her that . . . that you're looking sick because she's making you sick with—"

"You," Christopher gasped. "You're making me sick."

"With longing. Sick with LONGING!" Michael screamed.

"With LONGING!" Christopher screamed. Half a dozen people turned around to stare.

"Maybe we should not have any more poetry right now," Rox said. "It gets you kind of excited."

Christopher nearly collapsed with relief. "Maybe we should get some air. I guess maybe I . . . need some air."

Rox took him by the arm and he allowed himself to be led outside. Outside, the night had grown chilly. But the air was fresh, at least, and oh, how he needed fresh air.

"There was something I wanted to talk to you about," Rox said, suddenly more serious.

The word 'talk' made him cringe. He tried out a shaky smile.

"There's this thing my dad mentioned. You know about the film festival, right?"

Michael put down the microphone and sighed heavily. "Man, that was work. Lucky you came back when you did or the jig would have been up."

Julia nodded. "Glad to help. We're in this together now, right?"

Michael thought for a moment. He didn't entirely like the sound of that. He hadn't chosen Julia Ardmore to be his partner. Not that it mattered. It was getting close to the time to pull the plug on the whole thing.

"Yeah, we're together," he said guardedly. "But it will be over soon. I guess I could have just let him sweat and fall apart back there, but if Rox is so hot for the poetry, I had to give it to her. The only problem is, later she'll be expecting the same thing from me."

"I'll loan you some books of poetry," Julia said. "As smart as you are, you'll have no trouble memorizing a few love poems."

The flattery did not escape him. He graciously returned it. "You're obviously not too dumb yourself. How do you know all that poetry?"

"Oh, I have a pretty good memory. I read it sometimes, when I'm thinking of Christopher," she said.

"Uh-huh," he said. "You really think he's that great?"

"He sure is," Julia said fervently. "I kind of feel

sorry for Rox, because I have to tell you—once a girl's been kissed by Christopher I don't think she'll ever be interested in any other guy. I know."

"Whatever," Michael said darkly. The last thing he needed was to listen to more fawning over Christopher. In his earpiece he could hear Rox telling Christopher that he was charming and a perfect representative of the local community. . . .

What? What was that about the local community?

"About time to go ahead and break this up, isn't it?" Julia said, glancing meaningfully at her watch. "Let's get this over with. I want to see the looks on their faces!"

"Okay, yeah, it is time." He grinned. "You know, you're different from what I thought."

"You're exactly what I thought," she answered.

"Let's do this," he said. But then something in his ear caught his attention. Had he just heard the name of Craig Maslow?

"Wait," he said, concentrating. "I'm just trying to listen to—"

Suddenly his hand shot straight out and he grabbed the dashboard so hard his fingers dug into the plastic.

"Yes! Yes! Yes!" he cried.

He keyed the microphone. "Tell her yes! Tell her yes, you do want to do it! Listen to me, Christopher, you wanted to know what you could do to repay me for all my help? This is it! The answer is yes."

★　　　★　　　★

130

"My dad just figured it would be nice, you know, to have locals help with some of the presentations," Rox said.

In Christopher's ear a nearly hysterical voice was screaming, *"Yes! Yes! Yes!"*

Christopher felt as close to hysterical himself as he had ever been. It was absolute mental overload. He was exhausted from trying to hear and replay everything Michael had been telling him, even as Rox had seemed to grow ever more demanding, and now she was saying something about the film festival while Michael was yelling his head off.

"What?" Christopher asked.

"Will you do it?" Rox pressed. "That was the question; can I tell my dad you'll do it?"

"You'll do it! You'll do it! You owe me, pal!"

"Yes, yes, I'll do it," Christopher blurted, without any clear idea of what he had just agreed to.

"Oh, that's great!" Rox enthused.

"YES! Good boy. Just one more thing: ask her if you can invite a guest."

Christopher furrowed his brow. What was Michael yammering about now?

"Ask her if you can bring someone," Michael insisted.

"Um, can I . . . can I bring someone?" Christopher asked Rox.

Rox smiled, but it was a different expression entirely from the earlier smiles that had reduced his knees to jelly. "You know, Christopher, I had a premonition that you would ask that."

131

"Hah!" Michael yelled. He slapped the dashboard. "He can bring a guest. She said he can bring someone." He turned to Julia, one big grin from ear to ear. "I'm in, I'm in. Yes! I'm going to the film festival."

"Great," Julia said, trying to look perplexed. "Now is it time to go and break up the happy couple?" she asked innocently.

"No," Michael said, obviously horrified at the thought. "No. Not now. We can't do it *now*. Rox is getting Christopher into the film festival, and he's getting *me* in."

"Yeah, so?"

He grabbed Julia's hand with both of his. "Do you know who's coming to the festival? De Niro. De Niro is coming. That actor who plays all the action roles . . . the cowboy guy . . . Dayton Hill. He's coming. Jeffrey Katzenberg is coming. Michael Ovitz is coming. But most important of all . . . Craig Maslow will be there, and I will be the friend of his daughter's boyfriend."

"Wait a minute," Julia said, "how does any of this help me?"

"You?"

"Yes, me. I'm supposed to be getting Christopher back, remember?"

Michael knitted his brow.

Julia could read his mind: he was trying desperately to come up with a good answer, afraid Julia would blow this thing for him. She was confident that he would come up with some clever rationalization. Michael Serrano was the smartest, most manipulative person Julia knew.

"No problem!" he cried suddenly. "It couldn't be better! See, the thing is to humiliate and expose Christopher and destroy his relationship with Rox, right?"

"Right . . . so?"

"So what better place to do it than *at* the film festival? In front of Craig Maslow." Michael cackled his evil laugh. "By the time that night is done, they'll *all* know the name Michael Serrano."

"Beautiful!" Julia enthused, and in her excitement she threw her arms around Michael's neck and hugged him close. Close enough that he could smell her perfume and feel the texture of her smooth cheek against his. For her part she could feel the quiver that ran through him—the reaction he could not suppress.

Yes, Michael Serrano was the smartest, most manipulative person Julia knew—apart from herself. They were going to be so perfect together.

Chapter Thirteen

THAT NIGHT CHRISTOPHER'S first dream involved a robot. The robot looked a little like Tom Servo from *Mystery Science Theater 3000*—an empty plastic bubble for a head and arms made out of limp Slinkys. But on the robot's head was a cowboy hat.

Someone Christopher couldn't see seemed to be shocking the robot with occasional jolts of electricity, so that suddenly the robot would jerk and twitch and cry out in pain. The cries of pain were a sort of gibberish poetry:

But, soft! what light has broken yonder window?
It is the beast, and Roxana is the one!
Stop, stop saying that!
Shall I compare you to a bummer day?
No, that's not what I meant to say!

Thou art more hairy and temperamental!
Who wants to see your fardels bare,
When I keep my bodkin under my hat?
What? Woody Woodpecker? Wal-Mart?

Christopher woke up in a cold sweat. He had never woken up in a cold sweat before. A cold sweat was something you read about in books, but here he was in it.

"That does it," he said to the darkness. "I'm putting an end to this. I can't go on lying. She'll have to take me the way I am or not take me at all. I'm not some robot."

Yes, just tell her the truth. That was the thing to do. The thought reassured him as he rested his head on his clammy pillow again. This wasn't right; that was the important thing to remember. A man didn't do the wrong thing just because it would get him what he wanted. That was the same kind of excuse every thief and liar and crook on earth used.

His father would have been ashamed of him. His mother would be ashamed of him.

The only way out was to tell the truth. The only way out was the truth.

He fell asleep and dreamed again. This time he was not a robot. He was a bull. He was the same bull who had thrown him in two seconds and then proceeded to butt him in the butt. He was in the chute, the narrow, confined area the bull was held in just before he was released into the ring.

Leaning over the fence was . . . not Rox. It was Eva

Gabor, but a younger Eva Gabor, and she was singing the *Green Acres* theme song in a heavy Hungarian accent. And yet at the same time she *was* Rox, in that way dreams have of being several incompatible things at once. She sang and sang, and at the end of every line she looked at Christopher, waiting for a response.

And Christopher opened his mouth and said, "Mooooo."

When he woke from this second dream, the clock showed 5 A.M. Normally he could sleep in a little on Saturday mornings. But he did not want to go back to sleep and have any more dreams.

Michael barely slept. He woke up finally at nine, ridiculously early for a Saturday. But he'd been jazzed all night, and he was still jazzed, although a little sleepy.

He was going to attend the film festival. He was going to the party afterward. He was going to find a way to put copies of his screenplay into the hands of major Hollywood power players.

And, as a side benefit, he was going to have Craig Maslow's daughter as his girlfriend. Maybe they would even get married, who knew? Married. And then Maslow would have an early coronary, and then, who would they get to manage the Maslow empire? Who indeed? Hey, why not Michael, the son-in-law and genius in his own right?

Excellent choice.

It made him almost delirious. It was as if the heavens had opened and showered him with every-

137

thing he'd hoped for. And why not? He deserved it.

He was drinking his third cup of coffee, ignoring his little sister, and deep into a fantasy involving the Lifetime Achievement Oscar and a still young-looking Pamela Anderson in full *Baywatch* red bathing suit, when the phone rang.

"It's for you," his little sister said. "It's a girl, so it must be a wrong number."

"Don't annoy me," Michael said to her. "Someday you'll be La Toya and I'll be Michael Jackson." He considered that for a moment. No, that wasn't quite right. "Someday you'll be Tom Arnold and I'll be Roseanne."

"Mom! Michael's hallucinating again," his sister yelled.

Michael grabbed the phone. "Talk to me."

"It's me. Julia."

The sound of her voice surprised him and made his heart skip. "Julia?"

"Look, we need to talk."

"We do?" He was instantly suspicious. "Why?"

"It's almost a week till the film festival. There are going to be phone calls between Christopher and Rox, and conversations at school, and maybe even another date. We need to be prepared."

The mention of another date made Michael want to crawl back in bed. The very thought was exhausting. An entire week of keeping up his role as the voice of Christopher's romantic soul. He sighed. "Oh, man, I hadn't really thought about it. I was just looking forward to the film festival."

"You have to get through this week first," she reminded him.

"Yeah, you're right. When should we get together?"

"In an hour. Somewhere private. I know a place. Swing by my house and pick me up."

Michael hung up the phone. Julia was right. There was still a lot of work to be done before this was over. He showered and shaved, then carefully dried and combed his hair. He considered the choice of clothing carefully. Not that he cared what Julia thought of him, but he didn't want to look conspicuous, wherever they were going. Somewhere private, she had said. Who knew where that would be? He decided on casual—Levi's and a raw silk shirt. A couple of dabs of Safari wouldn't hurt, either.

She was waiting out in front of her house, leaning back against the fence, eyes closed and face upturned to the sun. Her hair was loose. She had long light brown hair that tumbled over her bare shoulders. She was wearing a blouse tied at her midriff, a pair of shorts and sandals, and carrying a shoulder bag. For some reason Michael recalled the sight of her the other night when she had stopped to adjust her panty hose.

He stopped the car and leaned out of the window. "Hey."

She opened her eyes, a slow, almost sensuous action, and focused her almost clear gaze on him. She smiled a smile that was part smirk. Michael found himself becoming annoyed. "Ready?" he asked grumpily.

139

She came around and climbed in beside him.

"So, where to?" he asked.

"That way." She pointed down the road.

Twenty minutes later they were at the end of a narrow gravel road that Michael had never even known existed, let alone followed. They were at the river, in a tree-shaded spot. They sat on lush grass, looking over the sparkling river and beyond to the sheer wall of the mountains.

"What is this place?" Michael asked uncomfortably. The outdoors always made him a little nervous.

"It's just a place where I used to come when I was little," Julia said. "My grandparents own the land, so no one will be bothering us here."

"It's nice," Michael said, with as much sincerity as he could manufacture.

"Uh-huh. Well, we'd better get down to business, here." She slung the shoulder bag down on the grass and sat beside it, legs crossed. From the bag she pulled a pile of books. "Shakespeare, Elizabeth Barrett Browning, Millay, more Byron, a book of Japanese love poems, an anthology of romantic poetry, and . . ." She held up the spine to read it. "Oh, and another anthology of romantic poetry."

"Oh, man," Michael groaned. He flopped down across from her. "This is more poetry than I really need to be exposed to, you know?"

Julia shrugged. "I agree, but Rox seems to get all excited about it. And let's face it, you are not the most romantic person on earth, so you need professional help."

"I faked it pretty well, even before we got into quoting poetry," Michael said a little defensively. "You know, for supposedly not being romantic."

"You know, the thing that's most worrisome . . ." Julia said thoughtfully.

"What?"

"Well, what happens *after* Rox dumps Christopher? I mean, she loves him because he's so romantic, right?"

"Yeah?"

"And she's supposed to figure that since you were making up all the romantic stuff that you are the one she really loves, right?"

Michael narrowed his eyes. He had an instinct, a kind of warning system that told him when he was about to hear something he didn't want to hear. "Yeah . . ."

"So, how do you keep her believing that you're this big romantic guy? See what I'm saying? You have to be able to keep it up for weeks, months. Years."

Suddenly Michael felt very tired. "Oh, man," he said softly. "You're right."

Julia nodded. "So, see, you have a problem. It isn't enough for you to make *Christopher* sound romantic, you have to be able to do it yourself. Face-to-face. And then there's kissing."

"Kissing?"

"Yes, duh. Rox has already kissed Christopher. Even if you *sound* romantic—and that's going to be tough enough to pull off—what if you kiss like a wuss?"

A cold thrill of fear went up his spine. "You're

141

right," he groaned. "You're right. I mean, I kiss great, don't get me wrong, but . . . but what if it isn't great enough?"

"Can you even *say* something romantic, face-to-face?" Julia pressed.

He waved his hand angrily. "Of course I can. I can lie just fine."

"You'll have to mean it," Julia said.

Michael grabbed one of the books and opened it. He composed his face into what he hoped and believed was a romantic expression, and read:

When in disgrace with fortune and men's eyes
I all alone beweep my outcast state,
And trouble deaf heaven with my bootless cries,
And look upon myself, and curse my fate,
Wishing me like to one more rich in hope,
Featured like him, like him with friends possessed,
Desiring this man's art, and that man's scope,
With what I most enjoy contented least . . .

He paused to look at her with what he believed to be tremendous sincerity and lowered his voice to a more intimate, enraptured tone:

Yet in these thoughts myself almost despising,
Happily I think on thee, and then my state,
(Like to the lark at break of day arising
From sullen earth) sings hymns at heaven's gate;
For thy sweet love remembered such wealth brings,
That then I scorn to change my state with kings.

Michael closed the book slowly. He had been so good he had almost moved himself. So he was surprised and not a little angry when Julia instantly burst out laughing.

She laughed for some time. And when he thought she was done laughing, she started up again.

"Oh, Michael, Michael. That was so perfect. You and *that* sonnet."

"What's the matter with me and that poem?" he said tersely.

"Did you even listen to the words? It's about a man who is feeling he's not getting everything he should. That other people are luckier or better looking or richer or have more friends. He's feeling sorry for himself, see, but then he realizes that he has this woman who loves him. And because he has this girl's love, he is already so rich and so lucky that he wouldn't even change places with a king."

"Yeah. So?"

"For thy sweet love remembered such wealth brings, that then I scorn to change my state with kings," she quoted from memory. Julia smiled her half-smirk smile. "Instead of 'kings' insert the words 'Craig Maslow.' You have to admit—the idea of *you* thinking true love was more important than ambition—" She started laughing again.

Michael forced a laugh, too. But he was still annoyed. "Okay, that was a bad choice of a poem, all right? I don't exactly think it's all *that* hysterical. It doesn't mean I can't be romantic. Let me just say

143

this—I *am* romantic. Okay? And I *can* kiss at least as well as Christopher."

"Really? Huh, well, maybe you're right. Although . . . ." Her gaze drifted up, as if she were remembering. Her tongue slowly outlined her lower lip, and then she sighed. "He does kiss very nicely."

"Who? Cowboy Chris?"

"We *did* go out for a while, you know," she said. Again she sighed and squirmed just a little, a liquid, sensuous movement. "Hey! Why didn't I think of this before? I mean, I've kissed Christopher. I could compare the two of you and let you know if you . . . you know, if you measure up."

Michael made a laughing, snorting sound. "Oh . . . right," he said, for lack of anything more clever to say.

"Oh, come on," she teased. "You're not afraid, are you? It's just a simple experiment. It wouldn't *mean* anything."

"Afraid?" he asked shrilly. "Me? Afraid? I don't think so." He moved closer to her, close enough that the already warm day seemed to grow warmer. Close enough that his heart was making loud thudding noises, like someone swinging a sledgehammer. He swallowed twice. His mouth was dry.

He leaned close and pressed his lips against hers. Then he pulled back.

Julia nodded her head slightly. "That was fine," she said flatly.

"Fine? Well, look, that was just a warm-up." He leaned close again and this time really kissed her. She opened her lips to him, and the kiss went on

144

till Michael was out of breath and tingling from head to toe and feeling that his hair must be standing on end.

"Okay, now don't tell me that wasn't a good kiss," he said, grinning loopily.

Julia took her hand and patted his cheek. "It was fine, really. It was fine. Now let's work on that poetry a little more. I'm sure if you're willing to work at this, we can get you ready."

Christopher looped the rope over the horn of Roxana's saddle. He looked down the steep side of the gully. The trapped sheep was bleating insistently with an expression that contained absolutely no hint of intelligence. The other end of the rope was tied around the sheep in a complicated cradle arrangement that hopefully would not slip up and strangle the animal.

Christopher leaned out as far as he could over the edge, while holding on to the rope.

"Okay, girl. Back. Back." The rope grew taut as the horse took up the slack. "Whoa, girl."

He looked down at the sheep, who bleated pitifully, not at Christopher in particular but more at the universe in general.

"Okay, Rox, back. Back. Back." The quarter horse knew her job, having performed this maneuver or others like it many times. The rope tightened and the sheep began to slide and scrape and slither up the side of the ravine, bleating stupidly the entire way. At the top Christopher quickly unwrapped the rope, and she went scampering off to the rest of the flock.

Christopher coiled the rope, knocking away the dirt clods and mud that had stuck to it. He looked up at the sky. The sun was setting behind the mountains, and already velvet twilight was settling over the valley.

He climbed on Roxana and headed her toward home at an easy walk. The horse was tired, too. It had been a long day and she wanted currying and feeding as much as Christopher wanted a shower and a huge meal.

Just under an hour later Christopher walked through the front door of the house, into the smell of roasting chicken and vegetables. His mother was in the living room, with paperwork and bills spread out on the coffee table and the news on TV.

"Hi, sweetie," she called out. "How did your day go?"

"Fair," he said. He went over and kissed the top of her head.

"You got a call," she said. She looked up at him with a sly smile. "A girl."

Instantly he was less tired. "She say who she was?" he asked as casually as he could.

"Oh, I'll bet you *know* who it was," his mother teased. "Roxana Maslow? Would that be who you were expecting it to be?"

He shrugged.

His mother laughed. "If you think you can fool me with that silent treatment, you're mistaken. Roxana. Same name as that new mare of yours. I

146

guess that's just a coincidence. I should have figured it out earlier. I must be slipping."

"I best go wash up."

"She left a message. She said to tell you that you should come over tomorrow to talk to her father about the presentation." She cocked an eyebrow. "Presentation?"

Christopher hung his head and slowly let his head bang into the wall. "I was going to tell you. I guess I kind of agreed to go to this film festival thing. With her. Her father wants to let some of the local folks help out."

His mother glanced at the bills and decided they could wait. She stood up. "Christopher, that's the same night as the rodeo, unless they changed the date."

"Yes, ma'am. It's the same night."

She looked as troubled as he felt. "You know how I feel about bull riding. It's just about the silliest thing a man can do for fun, but just the same, I thought it was something you were set on doing."

He looked away and bit his lip. "Yes, ma'am. I am set on it. Only I said yes to this other thing when I wasn't thinking right."

His mother rolled her eyes. "I'm guessing this young woman is pretty?"

"She . . ." He hesitated. Then he said, "No, ma'am. She's not pretty. She's beautiful." He shook his head helplessly. "She's more beautiful than . . . more beautiful than the finest day, or the clearest starlit night."

His mother laughed, but kindly. "I see. A special girl."

"Yes, ma'am."

"Just the same, should you give up something you had your heart set on just to please her?"

Christopher considered. It made him weary all over again. "I don't know," he said. "I suppose you do things, when you care about someone."

"Yes, that's true enough."

"And I reckon you say things you shouldn't say, too, and make a dang fool of yourself."

"I've heard of that happening," his mother said judiciously. "Of course even if you care a lot about someone, you don't stop being who you are."

He looked up sharply at his mother. How did she know? But of course she didn't really know. She was just talking in general terms. "How do you know where to draw the line? Between making someone else happy and being yourself?"

"Huh," his mother said. She wrinkled her brow. "That's a good question. I wish your father were here to give you the man's answer. All I can say is, people are who they are, and don't ever change very much. So you might just as well be honest with each other, because sooner or later the real person always shines through. No one can wear a mask for long."

Christopher winced. He knew it was the truth, but it was not what he wanted to hear. "Best get some of this trail dust off me," he said.

"By the way," she called after him. "She wanted you to call her back."

148

Christopher sighed. No problem—call Rox. Only first, call Michael. Michael Serrano, the mask he had already worn too long.

Rox hung up the phone. Once again Christopher had showered her with poetry and mush till she thought she might lose her mind. But, she reminded herself, somewhere, down under all that flowery talk, he was still the same person he'd once been. And, hard as it was to imagine, she knew Christopher was doing all this because he thought it was what she wanted.

She was convinced that the *real* Christopher was still the same blushing, stammering, sweet guy who had stopped to pick her up by the side of the road. All she had to do was find a way to get back in touch with his truer nature. Which meant, she supposed, that he would have to get over whatever insecurity drove him to try to sound like a gigolo from the court of Louis XIV. Insecurity no doubt being fed by a certain snake by the name of Serrano.

What on earth Julia Ardmore saw in him was a mystery to Rox. But Julia wanted him, and together she and Rox had come up with a plan to outsmart the boys at their own game.

She sighed, picked up the phone again, and dialed a number. It was time to push this whole thing to a conclusion.

A few minutes later she trotted down the stairs. She found her father in the screening room, watching rushes from a movie his company was shooting in Zimbabwe.

"Hi, sweetie," her father said.

Rox plopped onto a seat beside her father. She began talking to him, but a sudden trumpeting of elephants on the screen wiped out her words.

"Wait a minute," Mr. Maslow said. He raised his voice and yelled, "Kill it, Johnny," to the projectionist. The movie flickered off and the lights came on.

"Now what were you saying?" her father asked. "What was it you wanted?"

"I hadn't gotten to what I wanted yet; I was still in the buildup where I tell you how great you are and how generous and so on," Rox said.

"Skip the buildup and just ask," he said with a laugh. "You never ask me for anything. You know whatever it is . . ."

"It's kind of big," Rox said. "You'd have to fly someone in from Hollywood."

"Who do you need, baby?" her father said, doing a parody of the big-shot movie executive. "Brando? Costner?" He snapped his fingers. "No problem."

"Actually, it isn't *that* big a request."

"Thank goodness," her father said dryly. "Brando hates me."

"I have this . . . this thing. It's kind of like a science project, almost," Rox said. "I guess what I need is just a little technical assistance. I need a small amount of Hollywood magic. I think maybe I need Mr. Corelli."

Chapter Fourteen

THE ULTIMATE TEST was upon him. There would be no more minor skirmishes. Tonight was the Big One.

His room was a war room, Michael had decided. He had prepared for this night like a general planning the greatest battle of his career. Only instead of maps and battle plans, his room was filled with books. He had emptied the poetry section of the town library and the school library. He had books of plays. He had books of romantic quotes. He had song lyrics. He was certain that there was more concentrated romantic mush in his one room than in the entire remainder of the state.

He had read and skimmed and recited and earmarked until he was bleary. And from each source he had collected the best bits. These he had entered in his laptop computer, arranged by category—

Poetry (general); Compliments (with subcategories on hair, eyes, skin, general appearance, and clothing); Love (with subcategories headed "Love, in general," "My love," "Your love," and "Love of country and family," just in case they came up).

Now, with a click of a mouse, he could pull up the combined creative output of two centuries' worth of writers on the subject of romance.

"Okay, test me," he challenged Julia. She was leaning back against the edge of his desk, just beside him. Julia had suddenly received an invitation to act as one of the local presenters at the festival—just like that, with no finagling or manipulating or anything. It seemed mightily unfair to Michael, who had to go through this endless charade just to get in the door.

Julia was wearing the dress she'd chosen for the film festival. It was a simple enough dress, no fancy frills or anything. Just dark red fabric of some kind. He supposed it was appropriate to the occasion, though he was no expert on dresses. He did wonder just a bit if there might not be a design flaw, though—the neckline was cut rather low, and there wasn't any kind of back on the thing, and it was all held in place by two little strings that seemed certain to slide off sooner or later. Not that it was any concern of his, but the whole thing was distracting, at a time when they really should be concentrating on the business at hand.

"Come on," he repeated impatiently, "test me."

"Okay," she said. "I say, 'It's a beautiful night out'; you say—"

Michael punched the keys of his laptop. "Okay," he said. "'Silently, one by one, in the infinite meadows of heaven, blossomed the lovely stars, the forget me nots of the angels.'" He pumped his fist. "Longfellow. Yes! He shoots, he scores! Give me another."

Julia thought for a moment. "Okay. . . . I say, 'What do you think of my dress?' And you say—"

"Well, here's where we have to be smart. See, we can't have our boy spouting nothing but quotes all night, right? So we give him something simple yet effective." He punched the keys and read off the screen, "It's wonderful, though it is just the frame for a transcendent work of art."

Julia nodded. "That's very good."

Michael beamed. "Thanks. Last time I used, 'It takes my breath away.' I needed something new."

"And when Christopher says it, it'll really sound dashing and romantic."

Michael stopped beaming. "Well, it is dashing and romantic. Simple yet dashing and romantic, and *I* wrote it, not some dead poet."

"I said it was nice," Julia said. She leaned over and looked at the screen. Her dress leaned with her.

"I have other choices, too," Michael said, carefully *not* looking in her direction and thus remaining completely unaffected by any visual distraction like the hint of black lace that showed just a little. "Look at all these." He scrolled down a list of possible responses on the question of clothing and on into various other topics. "Is it hot in here?"

"I don't find it hot," Julia said. "That's a good one," she said, pointing with her finger and accidentally brushing her shoulder against his cheek.

Her skin was amazingly soft. He gritted his teeth. "'Soul meets soul on lovers' lips.' Yeah, that would be a good one right before they kiss. Soul meets soul on lovers' lips. That's Shelley, just in case you care."

Julia laughed a little. "See, Shelley knew."

"He knew what?"

"That soul meets soul on lovers' lips," she said.

It was the *way* she said it, Michael thought darkly—just that hint of condescension. "Is that supposed to mean something to me?" he demanded.

"What?" She had been scrolling ahead. "Oh, just what we were discussing last week. You know, when you were practicing kissing. I mean, that's the big problem, right? No matter what else happens, what if, between Rox and Christopher, soul has already met soul, and then you come along—" She giggled a little at the prospect.

"Yeah? What *if* I come along? What, my soul can't meet her soul? Is there something the matter with my soul?"

"No, no, no, of course not," she said, pressing a comforting hand on his hand as it rested on the keyboard. "Just because you may not be Christopher . . ."

"Man!" he exploded suddenly. "What has happened to the air-conditioning in this room? There's like no air." He stood and folded up the computer. "It's time. Let's get this show on the road."

"Wait," she said. "Before we go." She stepped close to him. So close that her foot accidentally pressed against his. She reached up with both hands, a strange, compelling, focused look in her face. He avoided meeting her eyes. They scared him a little. She reached both of her hands around his neck, drawing him down toward her, down till he could feel the wisps of her hair, featherlight, tickling his face, until he found himself marveling at the smoothness of her shoulders, the gentle, fascinating swell—

She straightened his collar and stepped back.

"Okay," she said. "Let's go."

"Urngh," Michael said, a strange, nonverbal, plaintive sound.

"What did you say, Michael?" Julia asked innocently.

"I said, yeah, let's go."

Christopher sat in the front seat of his truck, dark but for the green glowing dashboard gauges, staring at the device. It was on the seat beside him, a small square box, no bigger than a pack of cigarettes, with a long, thin, flesh-toned wire and a tiny earphone.

The device.

He was parked just a few hundred yards down the private road from the Maslow house. The house was brilliantly lit, spotlights all around, as well as light blazing forth from windows in every shape from square to semicircular to triangular.

In there, in those lights, in that mansion, she waited—Rox Maslow, daughter of Craig Maslow, all-powerful Hollywood potentate, number fourteen on the *Forbes* list of the wealthiest people.

Waited for him—Christopher MacAvoy, son of Edward MacAvoy, deceased, a rancher and sometime rodeo cowboy, and Darlene MacAvoy, rancher and housewife.

And then there was the device. He could throw it out the window. He could do it right now. And he could be just what he was—a simple enough guy who knew a fair amount about ranching and not much yet about bull riding and absolutely nothing about how to keep a girl like Rox Maslow interested in him.

In any case, this was not the night to be on his own. Not when he was facing a crowd of Hollywood people on top of having to face Rox.

He unbuttoned his starched white shirt and slipped the box into the waist of his good pants. Then he stuck the earphone in his ear, up under his hair, and rebuttoned his shirt.

"You there, Michael?" he asked wearily.

"Right here, my man," came Michael's voice, tinny and distant.

"Where are you?"

"We're parked over on the county road."

"We?"

"I meant me. You ready to go in and get her?"

Christopher sighed. "I was going to be over to the rodeo tonight," he said wistfully.

"Yeah, I know. I've been hearing about that stupid rodeo all week. You can ride a bull in the lousy rodeo any day, cowboy."

Christopher smiled sadly into the night as he started the truck's engine. "Naw," he whispered so low he hoped Michael couldn't hear. "I'd have to be a man to rodeo."

The town of Longhorn was unusually bright and busy. For 363 days out of the year, nothing much went on. Then, during two short days, the population doubled, the streets filled with cars, searchlights swept the night sky, pedestrians jammed the nearly nonexistent sidewalks, and lines snaked out the door of every restaurant and saloon.

At the far west end of town was the theater Craig Maslow had built to house his film festival, the two-year-old Orpheum, a theater designed to look like an old-time one-screen movie theater. Inside, it was many times larger than it seemed from the outside. It had four separate movie theaters, a banquet hall, dressing rooms, a full kitchen and pantry, and a bar.

For the three days preceding the final weekend, the theaters had been busy showing the twenty-eight films that had been entered in the festival, often to audiences of only three or four people, at other times to groups of a hundred or more.

At the far east end of town was the aging, decrepit

Bobby John Williams Auditorium, an oversized Quonset-hut-like building. The Williams Auditorium was used for parts of the county fair and for tractor pulls and rodeos. Inside, bleachers lined both sides, fronted by billboards advertising Western wear and snuff and Dodge trucks, around a dirt floor. At one end was what looked like a maze of steel fence posts, the holding pens and gates for the calves, the broncs, and the bulls.

Outside of the auditorium was a circus of tractor-trailers and Winnebagos, all the cowboys and stock contractors and vendors who went with the rodeo. Here, too, searchlights swept the sky, occasionally meeting and intersecting with the lights from the film festival across town.

Christopher had to take an unusual route in order to arrange to pass by the auditorium. He had debated the issue with himself while he was driving to town and mouthing the silly romantic nonsense that Michael was busily feeding him. He had told himself he didn't really even want to see the rodeo crowd and be reminded that tonight, the night he had hoped to be in there with them, he would instead be playing puppet for Michael Serrano and hanging out with the Hollyweirdos.

And yet he couldn't entirely stay away. It was an almost masochistic need to confront himself with the clear and convincing evidence of his own weakness. He pulled the truck to the side of the road and gazed out through the windshield like a toddler at the toy store.

"I talked to my dad about changing the weekend of the film festival next year," Rox said. "You know, so it wouldn't conflict with the rodeo."

Michael said something in Christopher's ear that, for once, Christopher ignored. "Yeah," was all he said. He watched as the stock contractors' men unloaded a big yellow bull from a truck, coaxing the huge beast down into the holding pen.

"Too bad you have to miss the rodeo," Rox said.

"How could I be missing anything," Michael said in his ear, *"when I am spending the evening with an angel?"*

"I reckon I'll catch it next year," Christopher said glumly. He tried to force a smile. "Besides, how could I say I'm missing anything when I'm having an evening with an angel?"

Rox made a quirky little half smile. "How indeed?"

There were valets outside the Orpheum, young men in red vests, red cowboy hats, and leather chaps. They looked ridiculous, in Christopher's opinion, and each of them would no doubt rather have been at the rodeo, too, but they were earning badly needed money. He supposed they were Hollywood's idea of cowboy types.

He pulled to a stop and climbed out. One of the valets, a guy named Terry Miller, came running around. "Oh, it's you, MacAvoy," he said. He shook his head. "What are *you* doing here? You got a job here, too?"

159

"You could say that," Christopher said glumly. He went around and took Rox's arm and, with sinking heart, led the way inside.

The lobby of the Orpheum was done in extravagant art deco splendor—soaring geometric shapes and curving chrome and golden light. It was filled to capacity with a motley assemblage of people—technicians on last-minute errands, running through with armloads of cable or lights; waitresses in very short white fringed skirts and tiny cowboy hats, weaving through the crowd, carrying trayloads of tiny bits of food on toothpicks and plastic tumblers full of champagne; and various important-looking, expensively dressed people, looking lost, confused, disturbed, drunk, happy, angry, or some combination of the above, while feeding from the trays of hors d'oeuvres and tossing down the champagne. There was loud conversation and loud music.

"Who are all these people?" Christopher wondered, retreating a little.

"Hollywood phonies," Rox whispered in Christopher's ear. Then she winked broadly and laughed, and Christopher laughed along with her, momentarily reassured.

"I would sell my little sister into slavery to be there right now," Michael's voice commented.

"I know that fellow over there from somewhere," Christopher said, indicating a short, bearded man with unruly hair and glasses.

"That's Steven Spielberg."

"Schindler's List, *Best Picture Oscar for 1993*, The Color Purple, *which was also great but the academy snubbed him, and* Jaws! *Don't forget* Jaws!"

Michael went on for some time, recounting a complete list of Spielberg's movies and concluding with the latest estimate of his personal fortune.

"I liked that movie," Christopher said, trying to tune Michael out.

"Which one?"

"Jaws," he said.

"I didn't mention *Jaws*," Rox said. "I'm so impressed at your knowledge," she said.

"Watch that," Michael warned.

"Too bad Michael Serrano couldn't be here," Rox said.

The sudden mention of Michael's name got Christopher's full attention. "Michael Serrano?" he repeated in a voice suddenly an octave higher. "Funny you should mention him. You remember I asked if I could invite a friend to the reception later? Well, it turns out Michael is the friend."

"You and Michael Serrano are friends?" Rox said, incredulous. "I'm sorry, but I can't believe that."

"Oh?" Christopher asked. "You don't like the fellow?"

"Don't like Serrano?" Rox said brightly. "No, that's not it at all. He's kind of good-looking, in a Christian Slater sort of way. Smart, too. Witty." She brushed her hair back off her forehead with a careless gesture that even now made Christopher drift halfway into a dream state.

"What else about me?" Michael's voice demanded insistently.

But Christopher didn't have to press her. "You know, I guess if you and I hadn't gotten together, I'd probably be going with him," Rox said.

"With Michael?" Christopher demanded, vaguely disturbed at the course the conversation was taking.

"Sure. The only thing is, Michael's not nearly as romantic as you are. He can't think up all the sweet and wonderful things you always say." She squeezed his arm close. "You will keep saying all those sweet, romantic things, won't you?"

Once again Christopher had the sense that something had just flown right by his head. There was a subtext in what Rox was saying. Information that was encoded in that way women had.

"Let's get backstage," Rox said brightly. "Daddy will be waiting for us there. And on the way you can tell me some more of those wonderful things."

In the car, down the street two blocks, Michael grinned.

"This is going to be easier than I thought," he said. "Listen to her! She's already halfway there. All she needs is to see the truth, and she'll be ready to dump the Marlboro Man for me." He glanced at Julia, sitting beside him. "And then, of course, he's all yours."

"That's the plan," Julia said with cool, restrained excitement. "It's working beautifully. By the time this night is done, you'll be with Rox and I'll be with Christopher."

"Yeah," Michael said. "Me and Rox Maslow."

"And me and Christopher MacAvoy. Boy, am I getting the better end of this deal."

"You're what?" Michael laughed derisively. "Are you kidding? I'm getting a shot at a big-time career here. A year from now I could be getting small parts in movies, plus my first screenplay will be going into production. I may not even need to go to college."

"And you'll have Rox Maslow," Julia reminded him.

"Sure, that, too," he agreed. "Whereas, what do you get? Christopher? I mean, seriously. I almost feel bad because I'm getting everything."

"Mmmmm, not everything," Julia said, practically purring in a way that incensed him because it was so . . . so . . . so totally unprofessional. It was childish.

"Yeah, Cowboy Chris," he sneered. "Big whoop."

"You just don't get it, do you?" she said pityingly. "Once I was kissed by him, I was ruined for all other guys. I mean, figure it out—why do you think I'm going through all this to get him back? It's not like I have a hard time getting guys to be interested. I'm not unattractive, am I?"

"No," he allowed.

"I mean, I think I have a nice face. Nice eyes. Don't you think I have nice eyes?"

He nodded. "Sure. They're very . . . big. And nice."

"And my body?"

"Ex-excuse me?" he stammered.

"My body. You know, all the important parts. They're all okay, right?"

"Urngh," Michael said for the second time that night.

"So, the point is, if I'm going to all this trouble just to get Christopher, it must be because he's something really . . . really . . . really special. Right?"

"Yeah, well . . ." Michael said, unable to think of anything clever to say. He drummed his fingers on the dashboard.

"It's almost too bad, in a way," Julia said. "If circumstances were different, you and I . . ."

He waited, but she just let it hang. "You and I what?"

"Oh, nothing." She waved her hand dismissively. "I was just thinking that if you weren't so determined to hook up with Rox, and I wasn't so . . . hot . . . for Christopher, well, I mean, you and I have a lot in common. We're both smart. We both have a certain way of looking at the world—some would call it ruthlessness."

Michael nodded in agreement. The word "ruthless" didn't bother him at all.

"And when you think about it, boy! If you put

the two of us together, there's nothing we couldn't accomplish," Julia said. "In some ways it's like we are perfect for each other, because let's face it, almost any nice, sweet, normal guy I could end up with would . . . well, I'd end up running him ragged and ruining his life. And mine. I suppose in my heart I know that's what could happen between me and Christopher, you know? He needs someone gentler, more like him. Whereas you, Michael . . . I mean, if you didn't have to think about getting close to Craig Maslow, I'd probably be much closer to the kind of girl you really need. So, under different circumstances, who knows what might have happened?"

"Yeah," Michael said tersely. "Of course," he said with heavy sarcasm, "you don't even like kissing me."

"Did I say that?" She shook her head. "All I meant was that it was a kiss without any real passion behind it. I was just saying back when I kissed Christopher, well, then there was . . . heat. Now, if there had been heat between the two of us . . ." She pursed her lips in a speculative expression. "I guess if you really liked me, and I liked you, and there was some passion, some desire, some longing, some hunger, some crying need, some desperate intensity, some . . . heat . . . behind your kiss . . . well, then it would have been a great kiss."

Michael said nothing. He had momentarily forgotten how to talk. He wished Julia would stop saying the word "heat."

"I have to go," Julia said brightly. "You know,

165

the ladies' room. Can you handle things here without me?"

Michael jerked himself back to awareness. But even then he felt strangely unsettled, fuzzy. Michael listened to the sounds coming from Christopher's microphone, trying hard to concentrate with a brain that just kept repeating the word "heat" over and over again.

"I think he's just getting backstage," Michael said. "I'll be fine. He has his little presentation speech all memorized, and I doubt if he'll have to talk much before then."

"I'll be back in a few minutes, then," Julia said. She opened the door and stepped out.

Instantly the car felt cold to Michael.

Chapter Fifteen

BACKSTAGE AT THE Orpheum was twice the zoo the lobby had been. The beginning of the evening's festivities was only minutes away. The presenters (including Rox and Christopher) were being shepherded and organized by hyperactive men and women wearing radio headphones and carrying clipboards. They seemed to be hearing messages from nowhere and occasionally talked into their microphones, swearing and muttering and looking overworked.

Christopher had some sympathy for them. It was not easy to deal with voices in your ear.

Lightpeople were adjusting lights, soundpeople were checking sound, someone somewhere was hammering loudly, people armed with big powder puffs were chasing movie stars around and attempting to powder their famous noses, and one well-known actor was yelling that his toupee was on at the wrong angle.

Rox had Christopher by the arm and was dragging him from pillar to post, making rapid-fire introductions to people Christopher couldn't begin to sort out. He just kept sticking out his hand and saying, "Howdy, pleased to meet you."

In moments of relative quiet he could hear what sounded like a nearing windstorm building out beyond the heavy blue curtain—the audience was filling the seats. Hundreds of them. Mostly professional movie people. People who knew how to speak in front of large crowds without sweating rivers, like Christopher had begun / to do. Somehow, with worrying about carrying on the charade with Rox, it had never really occurred to Christopher that he would be speaking in front of hundreds of strangers.

"This is my boyfriend, Christopher," Rox was saying to a tall, beefy man with a receding blond hairline. The man extended a big hand to be shaken. "This is Ross Drake. He's a screenwriter."

Christopher was savoring her use of the word "boyfriend," when a New York voice interrupted his thoughts. *"Never heard of the guy. Forget him,"* Michael said.

"Pleased to meet you," Drake said.

"You know, Mr. Drake, I'll bet Christopher could give you some help punching up your screenplay," Rox said. "What with it being a romance."

Christopher began to form the words "Say

what?" when Michael supplied them for him. *"Say what?"*

"Oh?" Drake said politely. He peered closely at Christopher. "How is that?"

"Christopher is the most romantic human being I've ever known," Rox said proudly. "He always has just the sweetest things to say."

Christopher made a sickly smile and wished the ground would just open and swallow him up. It was one thing putting on this act with Rox . . .

Drake looked skeptical. "You'll pardon my saying so, but this young man looks like a real, authentic cowboy type. I mean, I'd expect this fellow to be roping and riding and branding, not tossing off romantic quips."

Christopher had only a moment to feel pleased that this total stranger had seen past the picture painted by Rox.

"Oh, no, no, no," Rox insisted. "He's a poet. Or at least he can quote them all." She nodded encouragingly at Christopher. *"Okay, just give me two seconds . . ."* Michael said in his ear. *"Okay. . . . She wants romance. . . ."*

"I'm sure Mr. Drake doesn't want to hear—" Christopher said, trying not to sound as desperate as he felt.

"Oh, but I do," he said.

"O, my love is like a red, red rose, That's newly sprung in June."

Christopher felt a muscle in his cheek begin to twitch. He smiled the sickly smile again. "Um . . . O, my love is like a red, red rose—"

"Burns?" Drake interrupted, obviously shocked. "You can recite Robert Burns from memory?"

"Um, yes," Christopher said, gritting his teeth.

"Well, then, go on, by all means."

"O, my love is like a red, red rose—" Christopher began again.

"Wait," Rox said, interrupting him. "There's someone else I want to hear this."

Christopher swallowed hard, hoping against hope that the red flush of embarrassment wasn't creeping up his neck. But his face felt hot, and his palms felt clammy, and he was pretty sure that he was beet red by now. And now Rox wanted still more people to witness him making a jackass of himself?

Rox was waving someone over, but Christopher kept his eyes firmly fixed on the floor, and so he did not see who it was. All he saw was the man's boots as he joined the group, and then he heard the voice.

"Hi, there, Roxana," the man said in a voice that Christopher instantly recognized, and then refused to believe.

"Hi, Mr. Hill," Rox said. "I wanted you to meet my friend, Christopher MacAvoy. He was just reciting some love poetry for us."

There was a hand thrust out within Christopher's small field of vision. He had no choice but to shake it. And any other time, on any other occasion, he would have liked nothing more than to shake that hand.

He looked up, filled with awful dread, into the face of Dayton Hill.

"So, let's hear this . . . what was it?" Hill sneered. "Love poetry?"

And then Dayton Hill looked Christopher up and down, and laughed.

"Dayton Hill!" Michael yelled into the microphone. "Man, even *you* must know who Dayton Hill is."

Where on earth was Julia? She'd been gone for at least ten minutes. That was a long time in the rest room. Even for a girl. Probably combing her hair. Or else putting lipstick on her lips. Her lips. Her lips.

If there had been some . . . heat . . . she'd said.

Michael slapped his own face. "Would you concentrate?"

Now Julia was going to miss Dayton Hill. It would have been more fun with her there.

"Wait a minute," Michael muttered. "What do I care if she's here or not?"

He keyed the microphone. "Okay, Christopher, let's load up that poem again for Mr. Hill. 'O, my love is like a red, red rose—Aah!"

Michael jumped at a sudden burst of static from the receiver. "What the hell. . . ."

He listened again, but he could hear nothing. Nothing. Not a sound. Nothing but faint static.

The connection to Christopher was dead.

*   *   *

Hill squinted at Christopher.

"Go on, Christopher," Rox urged. "I brought you here to show you off."

Hill squinted at him and smirked.

"He's just being shy," Rox said. "Really, he's so romantic you'd never even guess he was a real cowboy type." She laughed gaily.

There was a sudden burst of static in Christopher's ear, loud enough to make him jerk. And then the static was replaced by silence.

"Um, I don't think . . ." Christopher stalled.

"Come on, Christopher," Rox said, "just do it."

Christopher looked at Rox. She was, without a doubt, the most beautiful girl alive, and the thought of losing her stabbed him right through the heart. He would be the biggest fool on earth if he lost her.

"Rox," Christopher said, "I don't reckon I'll be spouting any more of that mushy stuff."

"What? Why not, Christopher?"

"I'm sorry," he said heavily. "But . . ." He nodded to Dayton Hill. "Mr. Hill will remember what John Wayne said."

"Five minutes, everyone!" a stagehand yelled.

"John Wayne?" Rox demanded. "He was no poet!"

"Maybe not. But he said, 'A man's gotta do what a man's gotta do.' And Rox, although I love you like I love life itself, this man has gotta get out of here."

Rox watched him go.

"So how'd we do?" Dayton Hill asked, indicating himself and Mr. Drake.

172

"You did great," Rox said. "Thanks so much." She caught her father's eye. He came over when she waved.

"It looks like Christopher won't be a part of the presentations tonight, Daddy," she said. "He has somewhere else he has to be."

Suddenly Michael's receiver crackled back to life. It had been off for five minutes. Five minutes during which time that dumb clod-kicking cowboy could have ruined everything!

"Christopher!" he yelled into the microphone, "we were cut off. Try and give me some clues as to what's happening."

He heard the dull noise of the crowd, but no Christopher.

"Christopher! Are you there? What's going on?"

No response.

"Oh my God," Michael whispered to himself. "He can't hear me!" Rox was going to figure it out any minute now. Christopher would blow the whole—

And then Michael heard another voice. A voice that was not Rox.

"Julia?"

"This is so sneaky, hiding under the stage like this," Julia said, with a giggle in her voice. *"But I'd go anywhere to be with you, Christopher."*

She was with Christopher. Julia, *with* Christopher.

"How in hell did this happen?" Michael

173

screamed at the dashboard. He'd only been out of contact for five minutes, and suddenly Christopher was with Julia.

"*Kiss me. Kiss me again,*" Julia said.

"Kiss? Again?"

Silence followed. A terribly long silence. A terribly long silence punctuated only by what had to be considered a purring sound coming from the microphone, and the sound of blood rushing to Michael's head.

"*That was wonderful,*" Julia said breathily. "*You know what they say—'soul meets soul on lovers' lips.' Oh, yes. Yes.*"

At which point Michael threw the microphone in his hand against the windshield, cried "aaargh" loudly, threw open the car door, slamming it against the Porsche parked alongside, and hurled himself out of the car.

"You think everything is working okay?" Julia asked.

"If Corelli is on the case, it's working," Rox assured her. She looked around the room, a small dusty cubbyhole beneath the stage. From overhead they could hear the ceremony moving forward. Her father was telling a little joke, which was followed by appreciative laughter. "From what I could tell, he zapped the connection between Michael and Christopher at just the right moment. And right now Michael thinks he's listening to Christopher making out with you."

Julia held the small radiolike device to her mouth. "Oh, Christopher," she moaned. "You're so much better than Michael ever could be."

The two girls looked at each other and laughed.

"How long till Michael comes barging in here, do you figure?" Rox asked. She checked her watch. "I have to catch up with Christopher at the rodeo."

"Any second now," Julia assured her.

"You're sure he'll come?"

"Oh, yes, I'm pretty sure——"

With a loud crash the door to the little room flew open.

Michael stood there, framed by the doorway. Two security men were right behind him, panting as if they'd been chasing him.

"Get off her, cowboy!" Michael yelled.

He froze, warning finger still pointed, as his expression of rage slowly, slowly crumbled. In approximately ten seconds' time he went from bared teeth to slack jaw.

"That was fine," Rox said. "Very, very nice." To the security guys she said, "You guys can go. It's okay."

"It's better than okay," Julia said. "It's going perfect."

The two of them began giggling, enjoying the fact that Michael was still frozen in disbelief. He tried several times to speak, but his voice failed him. At last, in a hoarse whisper, he said, "You . . . you two set me up."

"With a little technical assistance from a guy

175

who works for my dad," Rox said. "It was fairly simple for him to monitor your frequency tonight and then, at just the right time, blank out your signal and substitute our own special recording. Corelli's a whiz at these things."

"You . . . set me up," Michael repeated stupidly. "But why?" He turned on Julia. "Why would you go along with her?"

"Julia didn't go along with me," Rox said. "This was all her idea."

"To get Christopher?" Michael asked, confused.

Julia sighed and stepped forward. She put her arms around his neck. "No, you fool. To get *you*."

"Me?"

Julia shrugged. "I know, I know. You have the morals of a snake and the ethics of a used car salesman."

"Amen," Rox agreed.

"But I guess I kind of like that about you," Julia said. "You're so rotten you're kind of cute. And after all, when you really started to think I was going to end up with Christopher, you rushed in here, bellowing and screaming."

"I was . . ." Michael thought fast. "I was . . . just seeing why the radio link wasn't working."

"Of course you were," Julia said. She kissed him full on the lips.

"I wasn't like . . . jealous," he said.

She kissed him again. "I know, Michael. I know. You have no feeling for me whatever. You're still rotten and self-serving. You're still bent on total world domination."

"Damn right," he said. And this time he kissed her. With heat.

Rox sighed. "I can't believe I'm witnessing this," she said. "On one level it's kind of sweet. On another level I have the feeling I'm witnessing the union of Darth Vader and Cruella De Vil."

Both Julia and Michael laughed, high-pitched, disturbing laughs.

Chapter Sixteen

H IS NAME WAS Danny Oh Boy. He was a yellowish tan color. He weighed just about a ton. His left horn was cut short, just a stump. He had not been ridden successfully in ten tries. Just a week earlier at Bullnanza he had thrown Terry Don West.

When it came to bull riding, Terry Don West was just about the best there was, while Christopher . . .

Christopher sat straddling the fence railing, feeling ridiculously conspicuous in the fancy clothes he had worn to the film festival. The bull was just inches away, snorting and heaving against the railings and generally giving the impression that he was not even slightly impressed by Christopher.

"You're up," one of the old cowboys said, and spit a stream of tobacco juice out of the side of his mouth.

"Yep," Christopher said. He climbed gingerly down, straddling the back of the impossibly huge, insanely powerful animal. Coming into contact with the bull was an electric feeling, like tapping into a high-power line. He wound the rope carefully around his gloved hand and pounded it with his free hand, making sure the rope was well seated.

His mouth was dry. His heart was pounding. But then he had become used to feeling afraid. At least here, now, he was afraid of something real.

The auditorium was loud with the voice of the announcer and the encouraging cheers of the spectators. The air smelled of cattle dung and leather and cigarette smoke. This was where he belonged, he realized.

It was all so simple here. So basic. No Michael yammering in his ear. No pretending, no phoniness. The bull was real. Very, very real.

He focused down, emptying his mind of all distractions. He slammed his hat down on his head, tested his grip on the rope, took several deep breaths, and said, in his best laconic cowboy voice, "'Spect I'm as ready as I'm going to get."

He bore down hard, narrowing his attention down onto the single matter of riding the bull, staying on his back for eight seconds.

"Christopher!" a voice cried out.

Rox!

He turned to look, all concentration lost as the thought flashed in his mind that she had followed him. Despite everything, she had come!

180

The gate was open.

Danny Oh Boy heaved, a bounding leap out. Christopher felt himself lifted up. His free hand flew back, high in the air.

He really, really needed to concentrate.

Boom! The bull reared and kicked. Boom! again. It was like riding a series of explosions.

The bull turned left, just like he usually did, and Christopher tried to stay inside the spin. Boom! A jerky, insane, bucking, twisting turn back to the right.

Christopher fought the urge to use his free hand to hold on. He was up, practically flying free. Then he was slammed down against the bull's back. And again and again. His jaw slammed shut, making his teeth rattle. His eyes felt like they might pop out of his head with one more good—

Boom! The bull caught him by surprise. He fought for balance, slipping to the side. The ground jumped up at him, dropped away, jumped up to get him again.

From far away the sweetest sound in the world—the buzzer.

The second sweetest—he also heard her voice, a wild, very-nearly-Montana-like *Whoop!*

Of course the bull didn't care that the eight seconds were up. He came clear off the ground, all four hooves in the air.

The pickup rider was coming in for the dust-off, but it was too late. Christopher's balance was hopelessly off now. Boom! He went flying, a weird, timeless feeling, like floating in water.

Then he hit the ground. He looked around, stunned stupid. The bull lowered his head and aimed his horns at Christopher.

Christopher jumped to his feet, just as the rodeo clown, dressed in clown regalia, raced through and distracted the bull.

Christopher picked his hat up from where it had fallen and dusted off his pants. He walked shakily off the field.

Someone came rushing at him and he flinched.

"Are you all right?" Rox demanded, looking him over for evidence of broken bones.

"Shook up is all," Christopher said.

"I'm sorry you fell off," Rox said.

Christopher grinned. "No, that was a good ride." He squinted toward the scoreboard. "Seventy-four." The number, though it was only a decent score, was still a sweet vision.

"You're telling me that's how it's supposed to be?" Rox said. "And this is your idea of fun?"

Christopher looked at her and nodded slowly. "I have a lot I have to tell you, Rox. The first thing is—all that romance stuff? That just isn't me."

"Really?"

"No." He shook his head for emphasis. "It's a long story, but the short way to tell it is that, well, this is me." He waved a hand around at the rodeo. "I'm just a simple, everyday fellow. Don't have much money. Probably won't ever, what with ranching for a living. I work hard, and getting

182

knocked on my behind by a bull is my idea of fun, and the fact is I don't always have a lot to say. So, see, the thing is . . . The thing is, I guess you'll have to take me for what I am or not take me at all."

"Well, it's about time," Rox said.

"About time for what?"

"About time you stopped thinking you had to pretend to be someone else. It's you I always liked," Rox said. "You. *Not* the voice of Michael Serrano."

Christopher stopped dead in his tracks. "You know about that?"

"I've known about it for a week at least and suspected it even earlier. It's a long story."

"For a week?" he demanded. "You let me . . . you let me . . . with Mr. Hill and all?" Then he laughed. "Hey. You planned it."

"Guilty," she said. "I knew sooner or later you'd reach the point where you just couldn't take it anymore. I knew you'd have to let the real Christopher come out, and that's the Christopher I love."

"Love?" he repeated wonderingly. "Even after all . . . after what I did and all? After I was a jerk? You l-l-l . . . You know."

"Love," she said again. "Yes, even after everything."

For several seconds Christopher found he was unable to speak. But Rox waited patiently as the words forced their way from his brain down to his mouth. "I love you, too, Rox." Then he grinned. "And that was me talking, not Michael Serrano."

They started to walk away, arm in arm, when

Christopher stopped her. "One thing I have to tell you, though," he said. "I . . . I may not always be able to say how much I love you; I'm not good with words. I guess you've figured that out by now. But I'll always feel it inside. And I'll always try and show it."

Rox kissed him, and from far off came the appreciative cheers of the crowd.

"And one other thing," Christopher said. "Since we're being honest and all. . . ."

"Yes?"

"Rox, I can tell the difference between a real flat tire and one that's just had the air let out of it."

Do you ever wonder about falling in love? About members of the opposite sex? Do you need a little friendly advice but have no one to turn to? Well, that's where we come in . . . Jenny and Jake. Send us those questions you're dying to ask, and we'll give you the straight scoop on life and love in the nineties.

DEAR JAKE

Q: *I'm eighteen years old and have a major problem. I've been going out with my boyfriend for eleven months now and everything is great when we're by ourselves. But when we're around our friends, he totally ignores me or puts me down. Once my best friend yelled at him for the way he was treating me, and then he took it out on me! Why does he treat me this way?*

AT, Toronto, Canada

A: You deserve to be treated with affection and respect by your boyfriend *all* the time—not just when you're alone with him. It sounds as if your boyfriend is insecure about himself and his relationship with you. Putting you down makes him feel superior and in control.

Your friends may mean well, but *you* are the one who needs to talk to—not yell at—your boyfriend. Tell him that his behavior is hurting you and that if he doesn't shape up immediately, you're breaking up with him. This relationship is damaging your self-esteem, and if this guy isn't willing to accept responsibility for how his actions are affecting you, you're ultimately better off without him.

DEAR JENNY

Q: *Why is love so scary? There's this boy I like a lot and he's asked me out twice, but both times I've been afraid to say yes. I don't even know why he'd be interested in me—I'm so shy when I'm around him. I just know he's going to ask me out again. What should I do?*

JL, Heber Springs, AR

A: Love doesn't have to be scary. I know it's hard to open yourself up and allow another person to get close. But that's not unusual.

For now, don't rush into anything that feels uncomfortable. If you really like this guy, find a way to get to know him better without the stress of an actual date. You could go out of your way to talk to him at school, or casually invite him along the next time you go out with a group of friends. The key is to set your own pace. When the time is right, love has a way of sneaking up on people—even the shyest ones.

Do you have questions about love? Write to:

Jenny Burgess or Jake Korman
c/o Daniel Weiss Associates
33 West 17th Street
New York, NY 10011